Look for More Titles by Cassandra Chandler

The Blades of Janus
PACK
PROGENITOR

The Department of Homeworld Security
Gray Card
Resident Alien
Business or Pleasure
Tied up in Customs
Entry Visa
Duration of Stay
Duel Citizenship
Invasive Species
Export Duty
COALITION RECKONING
Import Quarantine
Homeworld for the Holidays

The Forbidden Knights
FORBIDDEN INSTINCT

The Summer Park Psychics
WANDERING SOUL
WHISPERING HEARTS

LINGERING TOUCH

Other Works
CRAFTING A WRITER'S LIFE: Building a Foundation

Coming Soon

The Blades of Janus
PERIHELION

The Department of Homeworld Security
Nothing to Declare

Coalition Reckoning

The Department of Homeworld
Security
Book Ten

Cassandra Chandler

Copyright Page

This book is pure fiction. All characters, places, names, and events are products of the author's imagination or used solely in a fictitious manner. Any resemblance to any people, places, things, or events that have ever existed or will ever exist is entirely coincidental.

Coalition Reckoning
The Department of Homeworld Security, Book Ten
Copyright © 2019 by Cassandra Chandler
Print ISBN: 978-1-945702-42-6
Digital ISBN: 978-1-945702-41-9
Edited by Eliza Sinclair

First eBook edition: July 2019
First print edition: August 2019
10 9 8 7 6 5 4 3 2 1

cassandra-chandler.com
P.O. Box 91
Mission, Kansas 66201

Dedication

For the two Rays (Bradbury and Harryhausen)—
illuminators of my life's path.

Don't miss out on any of the alien action.
Subscribe to Cassandra Chandler's newsletter now!

Author's note: *These events take place before, during, and after Export Duty.*

Chapter One

Rich green foliage streaked past Brigid as the helicopter wove between mountains covered in pine trees. She hadn't caught a glimpse of a city, town, or even a road for a long time.

If she wasn't so worked up over her new job, she might have tried to sleep. The jetlag from being flown all the way to Montana from Australia was murder.

"Is this the only way to reach the lodge?" She glanced over at the pilot. "By helicopter?"

He grunted, which was about as much as she'd been able to get out of the guy. At least he was nice to look at— with short dark hair, Hollywood-style jawline, and a physique that made it look like his second home was the gym.

If he was one of the people she was supposed to cook for, she'd need to refresh her memory for healthy recipes. It had been a long time since she'd had a client who was into that sort of thing, and she wasn't thinking clearly with how little sleep she'd managed on the plane.

She only felt a little bad for leaving the trial-run as executive chef for the head of one of Australia's up-and-coming production companies. The guy had been hard to pin down on any specifics, and she already wondered if his offer had been serious.

The job she was heading for was solid, immediate, and came with a ludicrous salary. Brendan only needed her for a month, and was going to pay her more than she usually earned in a year. Sitting next to the silent man-wall, she was starting to question exactly what she was getting herself into, though.

There were deep lines etched between the pilot's eyebrows and he wore mirrored aviator glasses. From his bearing and how strongly he smelled of coffee, she had a feeling he worked security.

His button-down shirt was open enough to show off some of his chest hair. It also let her see the gnarly scar that ran over his shoulder and across his neck, disappearing beyond her view.

Maybe he was ex-military? He must have been through something terrible. She didn't understand how he could have survived such an injury.

The helicopter was raising almost as many questions as the pilot. For one, it looked way too heavy for the propeller blades to get it off the ground. Its body was made up mostly of big silver panels and thick windows that she was going to go ahead and guess were bulletproof. The landing gear things were huge and there were lights running along the length of them, unlike the simple metal bars that supported the few other helicopters she'd been this close to.

Inside, it was even more high-tech. The control panels were completely smooth, with a mix of regular dials and gauges and weird pulsing lights. Everything was the same silver metal, too—except for the barely padded black chairs. Her butt had fallen asleep ten minutes after take-off.

"I like the design etched on the panel." She reached out to run her finger over the ivy-like pattern.

The pilot grabbed her arm in a grip so tight it nearly hurt. He looked over at her and finally spoke.

"Don't. Touch. Anything," he said.

"My bad."

He let go of her arm, then ran a finger over one of the patterns. The etchings lit up, and the helicopter made a few beeping noises.

Shoot, are those part of the controls?

Brigid looked around more carefully, folding her hands in her lap and pulling her legs closer to the chair in an effort to not accidentally bump into anything.

A glass and metal dome appeared amid the foliage, with three large spans of roof spreading out from it. If this was the lodge, it was the strangest mix of futuristic and rustic she'd ever seen.

Finally.

They swung around and hovered over a small landing pad before setting down. She couldn't wait to stretch her legs—and to get out of this thing.

A tall, thin man with red hair and a neatly trimmed beard was standing off to the side of where they landed. He was wearing jeans and a burgundy sweater.

There was a woman next to him who was almost as tall as he was. She was absolutely stunning, with a huge smile on her supermodel-perfect face. Her hair was blonde, and she was dressed similarly, but her sweater was a clashing mish-mash of colors that no fashionista would be caught dead in.

Under her breath, Brigid said, "Yikes."

"Just wait."

The pilot couldn't have heard her, could he?

The engine noises weren't lessening, though they were quieter than she'd expected. They hadn't even needed those oversized headphones people always wore in movies when they rode in helicopters.

The red-head trotted up to the helicopter, ducking low under the propellers. One of the side doors in the back opened automatically.

As soon as he was inside, he said, "Hi, I'm Brendan."

This was her new boss? He was cuter than she'd expected, especially when he smiled at her. He reached into the cockpit to shake her hand awkwardly.

"Nice to meet you," she said. "I'm Brigid."

Brendan chuckled. "I know."

"Right." Of course he knew. He'd hired her and sent this man-wall to come get her.

Brendan turned to the pilot, and said, "Zemanni, turn off the engine."

"No." The pilot—Zemanni—shook his head. "Take your passenger and get out."

Wow.

So much for this guy being one of Brendan's security guards. She couldn't imagine anyone tolerating that kind of attitude from a subordinate.

At least Zemanni was rude to everyone and not just her. She'd been wondering if she had offended him somehow.

What the heck kind of name is 'Zemanni' anyway?

"You're not coming in?" Brendan smirked, obviously baiting the pilot. "Everyone will be so *torn up* to miss you."

Brigid didn't get the joke, and Zemanni didn't seem to find it funny. He turned to glare at Brendan. The lights from the dashboard were doing some weird reflecting thing on the white scar tissue around Zemanni's neck, because it almost looked like it was glowing.

"Get out," Zemanni repeated. "Or I'll take her back with me and you'll have to keep eating Dane's cooking."

Brendan's smirk faded. He nodded at Brigid and said, "We'd better go."

"Oh, sure." She managed to unbuckle her safety harness and climb into the main cabin of the helicopter with

Brendan. He picked up two of her bags, leaving her backpack for her to grab.

The moment their feet hit the white concrete of the landing pad, the door behind them slid shut. The trill of the engine increased, but was drowned out by a high, screeching roar that echoed through the forest. Brigid had never heard anything like it. She ducked down, heart pounding, scanning the trees and sky.

"What was that?" she said.

"That?" Brendan shrugged. "Probably a bear."

"A bear?" Her voice was shrill. She realized she wasn't using the best tone with her new boss, but couldn't help herself.

The helicopter took off.

Craaaap.

"There is no way that was a bear," Brigid said.

Brendan straightened as soon as the helicopter lifted off, and smiled down at her. "I thought I hired a chef, not a zoologist."

"My sister is a veterinarian." A familiar sense of pride flooded her chest, followed by just a little bit of envy.

Caitlin worked with all kinds of animals. She even assisted park rangers when they needed help with wildlife in the area around their home town in Arizona.

Cooking could be important, too, but Brigid mainly catered to people who were just seeking entertainment or distraction. Her experiments in molecular gastronomy were the only accomplishments she was really proud of. The people she'd worked for had always seemed more interested in showing off her cuisine than actually enjoying it. It was all politics and posturing.

"I didn't know she'd been trained in identifying bear calls," Brendan said.

He talked almost as if he'd already known what Caitlin did. Brigid was used to people checking references when she started a new job, but they usually didn't dig into her family.

She thought about the helicopter again and the military-looking guy who piloted it. Maybe she was going to have a chance to do something more meaningful after all.

The blonde woman approached them and took one of the bags from Brendan.

"It sounded more like a mountain lion to me." The woman extended her free hand toward Brigid. "I'm Vay. It's wonderful to meet you."

"You...too." Brigid was still giving most of her attention to the thick foliage around them. And crouching, she realized, as she looked up at Vay. Brigid forced herself to stand and tried to unbunch her shoulders. "Do you get many mountain lions around here?"

"Not really," Vay said.

"Then why do you think that was a mountain lion?" Brigid asked.

Vay opened her mouth, then shut it again and smiled, the

skin around her eyes crinkling.

At least she wasn't afraid. Brendan seemed unfazed as well.

"We should probably head inside," Vay said.

"That's a great idea." Brendan gestured toward the house. "After you."

What the heck have I gotten myself into?

Vay headed up a pathway of stone steps. Brigid followed, flinching at every snap of a branch or rustle of the wind. When they reached the lodge, she hurried through the open glass door, only letting out her breath when it was securely closed behind them. Hopefully, it was made out of some sort of reinforced glass as well.

How strong were mountain lions, anyway? Now she knew what she'd be talking to Caitlin about the next time they spoke.

"Sorry about that," Brendan said. "Zemanni isn't the most welcoming person, but Ari wasn't available to fly you in."

"That's fine." Brigid tried to regain her composure. "It was nice of you to send someone to pick me up at the airport."

Brendan smiled at her. "This isn't exactly a place you can find on your own."

Now that she was safely inside, Brigid could be properly awed by the building. They had stepped into a huge atrium. The walls rose up two very tall stories and the space was capped with the dome she'd noticed when they were flying in.

Two staircases hugged the walls across from them, heading up to a hallway. An ornate set of double-doors stood between the steps on the ground level, with gorgeous stained glass in geometric patterns set into their windows.

Small archways led off into two hallways opposite from each other near the main door. Another was right behind her, near the door that led to the helipad. A larger archway led to what looked like the dining room, from what little she could see of it. Everything was wood, stone, and glass —except for the metal frames for the dome above.

"Wow, this place is gorgeous," she said.

"Thanks." Brendan strode to the center of the space and looked around. "I designed this one myself."

"This one?" Brigid asked.

"Brendan has a bunch of houses like this." Vay stepped closer, that big smile still in place.

"They're not all like this," Brendan said. "Some are smaller."

"And some are bigger—like the one we're building in Florida." Vay rolled up onto her toes and bounced back down a few times.

"That's...great," Brigid said. She had no idea how someone could seem so excited to meet her, but Vay was staring at Brigid like a kid waiting to be unleashed on the presents at Christmas.

"Vay, don't you think you should go check on Henry and the others?" Brendan asked.

"Oh, right." Vay handed Brigid the bag she'd been carrying. "It's really great to have someone new around. I hope we can be friends."

Brigid had a strict rule about keeping up her professional boundaries at work—which also happened to be where she lived most of the time. She tried not to smile, but her mouth just wasn't listening. Vay seemed so earnest and sweet. And Brigid could already tell this job wasn't going to be like any of her others.

"Me, too," Brigid said.

Vay's smile deepened and her shoulders rose to her ears briefly. Brigid had never seen anyone so happy at the prospect of being her friend. It was hard to resist. Then Vay lurched forward and hugged her.

So much for boundaries...

"I'll see you around, then." Vay let go and stepped back, giving a little wave.

"Like maybe at dinner," Brendan said. "If we let Brigid get settled in soon enough."

Vay nodded. "I'll go check on Henry and...the others."

She cast an odd look at Brigid as she finished her sentence. What "others" was she talking about?

"See you at dinner." Vay smiled once again, then turned and headed briskly for one of the hallways.

"What Zemanni lacks in welcoming, Vay makes up for

about a million-fold," Brendan said.

"She's sweet."

And will take some getting used to.

"We can put these in your room and then I can show you the kitchen," Brendan said. "Unless you'd like to go there first?"

"Dropping these off sounds good." Brigid lifted the bag in her hand.

He nodded, then headed to the staircase opposite the hallway that Vay had taken. Brigid followed, trying to take in as much of her surroundings as she could.

The décor was minimal, but the place was still remarkably homey. That kind of thing could help Brigid gauge Brendan's tastes. Dark wood panels covered the walls, but there were plenty of windows to let in sunlight. And there was that ultra-modern dome.

A fusion of comfort food and some of her more innovative techniques, then. She'd have to ask about shipping in some liquid nitrogen.

Her feet sank into the lush carpet as she followed her new boss up the stairs and into another hallway. He led her to the end of the hall and opened the door on their right.

"This is your room," he said.

She stepped in and suppressed a gasp. A huge bed was nestled up against a wall that was mostly glass. The view was spectacular, and the linens were her favorite color— sea-foam green. She thought back to how Brendan had seemed to know details about Caitlin and wondered if it was a coincidence.

A desk and office chair were nestled under the windows. All Brigid would have to do was look up to see the mountains while working there. She had her own little sitting space, with a few overstuffed chairs surrounding a stone fireplace. There was even a fire already burning in it.

And it wasn't just a room—it was a full suite. She could see a large bathroom through an open door, and could only guess that the door next to it led to a closet.

"This is…" Her voice trailed off. She had no idea how to finish.

"I know, I know," Brendan said. "It's the farthest room from the kitchen. But I really think you'll be most comfortable here."

"It's wonderful. Amazing." She let out a brief laugh, feeling more than a little ungrounded. "I'm sorry. It's just so much more than I was expecting."

Brendan arched an eyebrow at her. "Even after seeing your salary?"

She felt her cheeks heat. "Especially after seeing my salary. I mean, *this* on top of *that*… It seems a bit much."

"I can afford it. And I really want this to work out."

Badly enough that he's giving me all of this and paying me a fortune just to cook for him and his friends?

Her stomach sank at the thought. There had to be more going on here than she knew. There hadn't been any mention of hazard pay in the huge contract she'd had to sign, but still…

"Dane is right across the hall," Brendan said. "Henry and Vay are next door, but they spend most of their time in the basement. I'm in the master suite in the other wing."

"That's everyone?"

He paused briefly, cocking his head to the side. "I don't understand."

"You told Vay to check on Henry and 'the others' earlier," she said. "But you just said the only other person staying here is Dane."

Brendan opened his mouth, then laughed and shook his head. "You're very perceptive."

"It helps in my line of work." Especially when she was entering a new situation. One that seemed way too good to be true.

"You'll primarily be cooking for myself, Henry, Vay, and Dane. Others may come and go, and I may need you to order special food supplies."

"Okay."

"I know this is kind of a strange job, but I can't stress enough that anything you see, hear, or do at the lodge is to be kept strictly confidential. The work we're doing is…"

"None of my business," Brigid said. "I read the NDA before I signed it."

Brendan continued his earlier statement. "The work we're doing is important. And we need to be able to focus and not distracted by—"

"Dane's awful cooking?"

Brendan's eyebrows hiked up his forehead. She hoped she hadn't stepped over a line, but from how Zemanni had used Dane's cooking as a threat before and based on how much Brendan was willing to pay her, Brigid could only imagine what they'd been dealing with.

"Your words," Brendan said. "Not mine." He gestured to the door. "I already ordered everything you requested, though most of it is in boxes in the kitchen. Shall I show you the way?"

"Sure."

He actually bowed as he said, "Your kingdom awaits."

Chapter Two

"Who the hell let the peanut supply run out downstairs?" Dane muttered under his breath as he walked briskly into the kitchen.

Henry and Craig could only keep Barbara calm for so long without her favorite treat. Her hormone levels were all over the place—not that he had any idea what was normal for a Lyrian in her condition. Or any sentient being in her condition, for that matter.

He pulled the doors to the main pantry open. Not good. The stacks of twenty-five pound boxes were dwindling, and his most recent order was running late. He leaned into the storage space, shifting the boxes around to get an accurate count of how many they had left.

Crap, he had to figure out what to make for dinner, too.

"Hello."

He started at the unfamiliar voice behind him, trying to leap back and hitting his head on the top shelf of the pantry. He grabbed the nearest can to use as a weapon as he turned to face the intruder.

A woman.

A beautiful woman.

Her dark brown hair was pulled up in a bun and held there with what looked like a stick. Her features were delicate and striking at the same time. Smooth skin, sharp nose, lips he wanted to reach out and stroke to see if they felt as soft as they looked.

She was small enough to be Sadirian—one of the Coalition's genetically engineered versions, like the soldiers he served with. He hadn't noticed her while she was messing with something in the cabinets under the kitchen island that dominated the center of the room.

She lifted her hands. "I come in peace. You can put down the beans."

"Beans?" He glanced at the can. 'Baked Beans' was written on the label.

Right. That's what they could have for dinner. Maybe he could boil some pasta to put them on.

He shook his head, trying to clear it, which only made the spot that he'd whacked throb worse, distracting him further.

"What are you doing here?" he demanded.

"Cooking? Or at least, getting ready to cook."

That didn't make sense. Dane was in charge of cooking. Not this…whoever she was.

She couldn't be Sadirian. Even with the height, she was all wrong around the edges. Her full hips would get her stuck in most of the tiny access tunnels on their ships or stations, not to mention trying to crawl through the small spaces with those…

How the hell does she stay upright with those breasts?

He was having trouble looking away from them. But this was Earth, and that was one of the areas he wasn't supposed to stare at. Right?

His thoughts weren't connecting right and his head hurt. He couldn't have hit himself hard enough to get a concussion, but all the stress of caring for Barbara and with the *Reckoning* on the way—it was getting to him.

And no regen bed in sight.

Not that he'd use one of the damned things unless he absolutely had to.

"Hello?" the woman said. "Are you okay?"

"Yeah, I'm fine. Just trying to sort this out."

The lodge wasn't being overrun by Coalition soldiers looking to take Dane and his friends into custody for daring to try to help Earth form a first contact committee without the High Council's approval, and she sure didn't look like the vanguard to a security force. That left…what? A lost Earthling?

"Who are you?" he asked.

"I'm Brigid. The new chef?"

"Chef…"

"I'm here to rescue you from Dane's cooking."

"What?" He lowered the can. "It's not that bad."

She snorted, but then her eyes widened and her mouth dropped open. "Wait. Are you Henry?"

"I'm Dane," he ground out.

"Oh crud. I'm so sorry." She scurried around the counter, hands clasped together.

Damn, she was short. And with his height and the V-neck sweater she was wearing, it made not staring at her cleavage that much harder. He forced himself to look at her face.

Big eyes. Another Sadirian trait.

But hers were warm, wide, filled with concern. They were the same rich blue of the deep ocean water the transport had flown over when he and his team arrived at the Florida base the Department of Homeworld Security was creating. He'd never seen that color in someone's eyes. Not in a fellow Sadirian's, anyway.

Her skin was pale, like she didn't get much sun—or had been stuck on a spaceship most of her life. It set off the pink of her lips and made the flush that was spreading down her neck and across her chest easily visible.

He set down the can of beans.

Plenty of Earthlings didn't get much sun. Brendan was a perfect example. And just because this woman had the big eyes and short stature of a Sadirian didn't mean she was an enemy.

Besides, the Coalition of Planets didn't work that way. If they wanted to send in a spy, they'd use a shape-shifting

Scorpiian, like Zemanni. Earth's Department of Homeworld Security was just lucky that Zemanni had fallen for an Earthling and joined their side.

Dane doubted the High Council would bother sending another assassin, since they had already dispatched the *Reckoning* to "address the situation on Earth." He figured he and his team only had about a month to prepare.

He needed to get some sleep. He was seeing enemies everywhere.

"Are you okay?" Brigid asked. "You're just kind of staring at me. Or, you know…glaring."

Dane lifted a hand to rub the spot on his head, but flinched at the pain radiating from it. He hissed in a breath.

"I'm fine," he said. "I just don't know why Brendan hired a chef without telling me."

"He probably wants you to be able to focus on… whatever it is you do here."

"I'm a—" He stopped himself from saying 'med-tech', searching for the local Earth term instead. "I'm a doctor."

"A doctor?" Her eyes widened further. "Well, there you go. You must have much more important things to focus on than cooking."

He let out a snort, then remembered that med-techs on Earth were actually held in high esteem. Back on his original ship, the *Arbiter*, they had regen beds to handle everything from minor scrapes to life-threatening injuries. Even as an advanced med-tech, he was seen as a button pusher.

Nutritional engineers were much more essential, especially the ones who designed new and more efficient food sources for the many varied citizens of the Coalition.

His food wasn't *that* bad. Considering that he and Vay had only eaten nutrient bricks until arriving on Earth, beans on spaghetti was a feast.

But then, anything was a feast when compared to nutrient bricks.

"Damn," he said. "My cooking really *is* that terrible."

"I'm sure it's fine."

"No, it isn't."

"Well… I can teach you." Her mouth opened and closed a few times wordlessly, and she looked away.

"That's okay," he said.

"No, really. If you enjoy cooking, I'd be happy to teach you."

Definitely not a Sadirian agent.

He smiled at her. "Thanks. I'd like that."

She smiled back, the flush deepening on her chest and rising up to her cheeks as they stared at each other. If he didn't know better, he'd think she was interested in him.

He shouldn't be thinking about that kind of thing. There was too much at stake for him to let himself get distracted.

Her eyes brightened. "Hold on."

She hurried to the fridge and opened the large drawer at the bottom that held the freezer unit. She pulled out a bag of frozen peas, then shoved the drawer shut. She turned around, smiling at him with those lush lips.

"What am I supposed to do with those?" he asked.

She laughed. "Put them on your head. You know. Like an ice pack?"

"Those are peas."

"Yeah. And they're frozen."

"Why would that make me want to put them on my head?" he said.

"Come on." She narrowed her eyes at him playfully. "You've never used peas as an ice pack before?"

This must be some sort of Earth tradition that he didn't know about yet. He tried to play off his ignorance. "Well, I did just hit my head pretty hard."

She laughed again. The sound was so sincere—as was her expression. His stomach felt a little weightless.

"I thought you were fine," she said.

"I might be a little rattled."

She grasped his elbow gently, but her touch might as well have been from a shock cannon. He sucked in a quick breath as tingling energy tore along his nerves, making the hair on his arms stand on end and his dick start to harden.

No, no, no...

"Did you hit your elbow, too?" she asked, pushing his rolled sleeve farther up his arm.

He didn't know what it was about this planet, but members of the Coalition were falling for Earthlings faster than a ship going through a dropgate. Sadirians, Scorpiians, even a couple of Tau Ceti had pair-bonded with people from this planet.

Dane couldn't let himself get distracted. Not with the possibility of making so many new alliances right at hand —and with the *Reckoning* so close to ruining everything.

He tried to step away from Brigid, but she followed, a little furrow appearing between her dark eyebrows.

"Are you okay?" she said.

"I'm fine."

"You keep saying that, but you're not acting fine. I think you need to sit down."

She reached for his arm again, but he quickly lifted it, spinning out of the way. Her touch had felt so good, he wasn't sure he could keep his thoughts straight if she made contact again.

"I'm good," he said. "I can sit myself down."

He crossed to the small table that was nestled into a set of bay windows overlooking the forest and sat in one of the chairs next to it. When she followed, he held out his hand and wiggled his fingers, staring at the bag of peas she still carried.

She scowled as she handed it over. That was good. If she didn't like him, maybe he'd stop liking *her* so much. Because he had to admit, he already liked her quite a bit.

Aside from being really nice to look at, she was…nice in general. Considerate, empathetic, kind.

He could already tell that she liked to take care of people—something they had in common. And if that core reactor response to Brigid's touch was what Vay meant when she talked about her and Henry having physical chemistry, Dane could appreciate his colleagues' choices better.

It would be best if he minimized contact with Brigid. Maybe even proximity. Definitely no to the cooking lessons.

Damn, he really did want to learn how to cook, though. He let out a sigh as he gripped the sides of the bag of peas, preparing to tear it open.

"Wait." Brigid grabbed his hands to stop him.

Warmth spread up his arms, filled his chest, and flooded his belly. He imagined pulling her onto his lap, letting her straddle him. His dick was already fully invested in that plan. He could wrap his arms around her, crush her against his chest, taste those plum-red lips.

"That's not how it works," she said.

Tell that to the ones who've pair-bonded already.

"So, I'm doing this wrong, too?" he asked.

She stuck her lower lip out a little. He wanted to nip it with his teeth.

Dammit.

"Sorry." He shook his head and looked away, wincing at the dull ache the movement caused.

"It's okay." She stepped closer and gently set the bag of

peas on his head, right on the spot he'd hit.

The pain intensified for an instant, but then abated as his scalp absorbed the coolness of the bag. He closed his eyes and let out a slow breath.

"That's a really neat trick," he said.

"You sound like you've never used an ice pack before."

"I haven't."

She snorted. "And you're a doctor."

"We rely more on chemicals and high tech gadgetry where I'm from. I mean where I trained."

He quickly corrected his statement, opening his eyes to read her reaction. No sense getting her wondering about his origins.

"From that accent of yours, I'd guess you're from the deep south," she said.

So much for that plan.

His speech patterns had been designed to help him blend in with Earthlings who lived near the Florida base. They hadn't known he'd be needed in Montana.

Even though the entire team had received the new cultural programming, his was the only accent that really took. Maybe something about his adrenaline levels had made it stick, what with him being the only member of the team who knew just how extensive their programming sessions could be. Programming pods scared him even more than regen beds.

He somehow couldn't bring himself to lie to Brigid, so

he settled on, "Sounds so, doesn't it?"

She narrowed her eyes at him again, but was smiling. "Well, a painkiller wouldn't be a bad idea. I could get you one, if you'd like. I have some in my bag." She gestured to a large backpack that was leaning against the kitchen island.

Dane glanced up at her. She was standing closer than before. Way too close. He didn't have any place to retreat to—and honestly didn't think he wanted to try.

"You gonna take that part of my job, too?" he said, smirking at her.

Her eyes widened and she opened her mouth, stammering.

"Relax, sweetheart. I was only making a joke."

Her scowl returned, stronger than ever, but he had the sense she didn't really mind his teasing. He hoped so, anyway.

Movement behind her caught his eye. The pantry doors were still open, and one of the boxes of peanuts floated out. Then another. And two more.

Craig...

"Is something wrong?" Brigid started to look over her shoulder, following Dane's gaze.

"No! I mean—"

He grabbed her hips and pulled her between his spread knees. She stumbled and landed against his chest. The bag of peas started to fall, and that, of all things, caught her attention.

She reached up and grabbed it, pushing it back in place on his head. Which left her sprawled on his lap, laying against him, face only an inch or so away from his, breathing just about as heavy as he was.

His arms were around her, just like he'd imagined. If he let go, she might fall.

Yeah, that's *why I'm holding on so tight.*

From the corner of his eye, he could see the boxes of peanuts suspended in the doorway as Craig undoubtedly paused and stared at them. The Lyrian's natural ability to camouflage himself didn't hide what he was carrying, and it looked like he'd tucked a box of peanuts under each of his four arms.

A deep, rumbling chuckle flowed through the room.

"Dammit, Craig," Dane hissed.

"Who's Craig?" Brigid twisted in his arms as she tried to turn to the doorway.

Crap.

Dane had to keep her attention on him and didn't have time to think. He leaned forward and kissed her.

The moment their lips touched, heat flooded through his body. His head spun, his skin felt electrified. He expected her to pull away, but instead, she barely hesitated before kissing him back. She let the frozen peas fall to the ground, gripping his cheeks with her chilled hands.

Dane pulled her closer, one hand sliding down to her ass

and the other gripping her neck to tilt her head to the side and deepen the kiss. She gasped, and he used the opportunity to slide his tongue into her mouth. She let out a little moan, tentatively meeting his explorations.

How had this gotten so far out of control?

Brigid shifted on his lap, bringing her legs to either side of him and straddling him. She pressed her chest against his.

He wanted to feel her breasts in his hands, in his mouth, under his teeth. Instead, he gripped her hips tighter, pushing her down on his erection. Damn, she felt so good.

The moan she let out was anything but little. He swallowed the sound, kissing her harder, plunging his tongue into her mouth. There was nothing on the table but some boxes—supplies Brendan must have ordered for *her* to use, not Dane.

He didn't care at the moment. All he cared about was that the table looked sturdy enough to hold their weight. He grabbed her ass and was just about to lift her onto it when someone cleared their throat.

Brigid jolted back in his arms. Dane held on to keep her from falling.

She twisted around to see Brendan standing in the doorway.

Brendan's eyebrows were about as far up his forehead as they could go. He cocked his head to one side, his mouth opening and closing as he gestured toward them.

"I…um…" Brendan said. "I see you've met Dane."

Chapter Three

Brigid flailed an arm as she tried to scramble off Dane's lap, half-catching herself on the table. Lucky for her, Dane didn't seem eager to let her go, and helped her stay semi-upright. She managed to get to her feet, quickly brushing the hair that had fallen in front of her face back behind her ear.

"Yes, we've met," she said.

She glanced down at Dane. He squirmed a bit in his chair and pulled at the pantleg of his jeans. Probably trying to give himself more space for—

Holy wow.

No wonder she'd been so carried away, grinding against *that.*

Oh my God. I was grinding against this guy I just met in front of my boss. In my kitchen. My workspace.

Her cheeks were stinging. They must be beet-red.

"I'm so sorry," she said.

Brendan shook his head. "Two consenting adults. None of my business."

"I promise you, sir, that won't happen again," she said.

Brendan shivered. "Never call me 'sir'. It's Brendan."

"Right," she said. "Brendan."

Brendan smiled at Dane, and said, "Henry was a little worried when you didn't come back with the peanuts."

"I was occupied." Dane's voice had dropped about an octave, and both the rasp and the sexy accent were even more pronounced.

Brigid shook herself, trying to keep her focus. "Peanuts?"

"Yeah." Brendan stepped further into the kitchen and peered into the pantry. She hurried to stand next to him, wanting to learn more about their culinary needs.

The pantry was half filled with twenty-pound boxes…of peanuts. Most of the lower shelves had been removed to make room for them. That must have been how Dane hit his head. The pantry was pretty deep, and he could have been leaning in to take inventory.

"I'm sure you're wondering why we have so many," Brendan said.

"I was actually wondering if the person who designed this pantry had ever used a kitchen." She remembered too late that Brendan had said he designed this house himself. "I can't seem to get my foot out of my mouth today."

Brendan just smiled. "I have to admit, the kitchen wasn't at the top of my priority list."

He reached in and picked up one of the boxes, hefting it

on his shoulder, then grabbed another and managed to pile it on the first.

"Let me help you," Brigid said.

"I've got it." Brendan shifted the weight of the boxes. "They're not that heavy, but they're awkward to carry. When you're done with Dane, could you send him down with a couple of boxes?"

"Done with...?" Her cheeks started stinging again. "I'm... That's over. I mean, it was a lapse in judgment."

"Hey," Dane said. "I'm sitting right here."

"I know, and I'm sorry." She felt bad, but at the same time, this was damage control. She shouldn't have been messing around with him in the first place.

"As much as I'd love to watch you two sort this out, I need to get back downstairs," Brendan said. "Just maybe don't get too carried away where we all eat and prepare food. Your bedrooms are right across the hall from each other."

"Great," Dane said.

Brendan nodded at Dane, and said, "Make sure you put in another order. We're running way too low."

"I did put in an order." Deep furrows had appeared between Dane's eyebrows. "It's late."

Brigid stepped forward. "I can help with that. Ordering food should be part of my job."

"That's a good point," Brendan said. "I'm sure Dane can get you all set up with that."

"Oh… Sure." Hopefully she'd be able to keep her hands off of him long enough to learn any quirks to their ordering needs. She smiled at Dane, trying to smooth things over with him. She really hadn't meant to hurt his feelings. "Maybe you can show me when we start our cooking lessons."

"Cooking lessons?" Brendan nodded. "That's a good idea."

"You could have told me I needed to work on it," Dane said.

"I suppose," Brendan said. "But then you wouldn't have had a chance to meet Brigid."

Dane just scowled back.

Brendan paused as he turned toward the door. Leaning a little closer to Brigid, he said, "And about that 'it won't happen again' thing—you shouldn't make promises you don't want to keep."

"I—" She stammered, trying to come up with a professional response.

"Your references said you're really big on boundaries," Brendan said.

"I assure you, I am," she said. "Usually."

"Yet you made a connection that crashed right through them." He shrugged his free shoulder. "Maybe you should give that some thought."

"I… I will." She glanced over at Dane. He was staring out the window, tapping the fingers of one hand on the table.

As Brendan headed out of the kitchen, he said, "Looking forward to dinner."

"Great," Brigid mumbled. She had no idea what to make.

With her new boss gone, she turned back to Dane. He glanced at her from the corner of his eyes.

"This isn't the best way to start a new job," she said.

"Forget it. I'm the one who got carried away and kissed you."

She felt a pang in her chest both from his words and his sullen expression. Broken boundaries or not, that had been the best kiss of her life. Even now, she was tempted to crawl back in his lap and pick up where they'd left off.

"Well, I'm the one who kissed you back." She smiled, hoping to ease the tension between them. His expression remained sullen.

Maybe another angle would help. She walked closer and said, "I'm still getting my bearings here. Any ideas on what I should make for dinner?"

"My ideas on food are what prompted Brendan to try to get me out of the kitchen."

"I like you here." She felt her eyes widen, her mouth dropping open. Dangit, what was it about this guy that slipped right through her defenses? "I mean..."

"Don't worry about it."

Dane lifted his hand to his forehead and rubbed at it,

shielding his eyes. She remembered she hadn't brought him those painkillers yet. She hurried over to him and picked the bag of frozen peas up from the floor.

"Here," she said, handing him the bag. "Put this back on your head and I'll get you those painkillers."

"No thanks." He tossed the peas on the table.

"They'll help." She picked up the bag and put it on his head herself, holding it in place.

"I was mostly talking about the painkillers. I don't use those."

She cocked her head to the side. "You're a doctor, yet you don't want to take medicine that will help you feel better?"

He snorted. "Not *that* medicine. I'll be fine."

"Of course you will. But you're suffering needlessly."

"That's the least of my problems right now."

"How can I help?" She shifted a little closer.

He arched an eyebrow at her, then let out a long sigh. She could feel the warmth of his breath rustle her hair. Maybe she'd stepped a little closer than she'd thought.

Dane dropped his gaze to her chest. Which was…yeah, way closer than she'd thought, but she had to lean forward to keep the peas in position without putting too much pressure on his head.

A muscle in his cheek started to twitch. His lips parted as he stared at her.

Then he looked down at her thighs, right between his

own. She was practically in his lap again. And his lap was still very impressively ready for action.

He glanced at the bulge in his pants, then back to her.

"Maybe you should think about baseball?" she said.

"What's baseball?"

She snorted. "Be serious. I'm trying to help, here."

"Standing that close and giving me this view isn't helping my situation at all." He looked at her chest briefly, then pointedly shifted his gaze away.

"Then you hold the peas in place."

"No thanks."

"You're not being very cooperative."

"It's not that I don't want to cooperate," he said. "If I take the bag, then you'll move away. And I'm not quite ready for that, either."

She was suddenly very aware of her heartbeat—the way it pounded on her ribs, as if asking her to open them so it could go to him.

What the heck is wrong with me?

It was just the sleep deprivation. She would get through dinner, have a good night's sleep, and tomorrow this would all be an embarrassing memory. She still wasn't sure what to do about Dane, though.

"About what I said earlier," she began. "I didn't mean that I regret anything. Or that I blame you or don't want to…you know."

He looked up at her, a wicked gleam in his eye. "Maybe

you should spell it out for me, just so we're clear."

She scowled at him. "This is my job. I don't want to mess it up."

"I know the feeling," he murmured.

"Brendan doesn't seem to care, though. About us... fraternizing."

"Is that what you call it?"

A dimple appeared in his cheek as his smile deepened. She wanted to run her fingertips over it.

"I have a strict policy about not getting personally involved with the people I work for or with," she said. "I'm just here to cook."

"Just here to cook? You're going to be living here and your plan is to what? Cook and hide in your room?"

That was what she normally did. Experiments in the kitchen, research in her room, and frequent calls to her twin sister, Caitlin. Calls that Brigid wasn't sure how to handle, with that strict NDA she'd signed.

"I read a lot," Brigid said. "I don't usually need much social interaction. The fact that I'm talking so much is just because I haven't slept in too long, so my boundaries are down and my filters are off—not that I would share anything I'm not supposed to when I'm tired, just... I'm rambling. I ramble when I'm tired."

He kept smiling at her. "You're cute when you're tired."

"You're...just...cute."

His low chuckle vibrated through her body, making her

toes curl. She really wanted to kiss him again or run her fingers through the sandy-brown hair that fell across his forehead.

He must have been feeling something similar, because he gripped her hips and pulled her onto his leg. She braced her elbows on his broad shoulders, trying to keep the frozen peas in place.

At least she wasn't straddling him this time.

He wrapped his arms around her waist and stared at her. "So, what are we going to do about this situation we have here?" he said.

"I don't know. I'm hoping I'll have more willpower to resist you after I sleep, but I've never reacted to anybody this way."

"I was talking about dinner, but if you'd rather talk about how irresistible I am, I'm up for it."

"Oh."

Was she ever going to get her foot out of her mouth? She didn't know how she was going to recover from all this —or if she even could.

After how badly her last job had ended, she needed to be at the top of her game. Higher than that. Instead, she'd humiliated herself in front of her new boss and thrown herself at a near total stranger.

Except, no one but her seemed to mind. In fact, Brendan had given her that really sweet bit of advice before he left. And Dane...

Dane really was irresistible. She'd only be around him for a month, and then she could go back to her routine and her boundaries and her normal workaday life.

She let go of the bag with one hand so she could run her fingers over the dark stubble on his cheek. There was a lot of it. His scruffy hair was long enough to brush his shoulders. She wondered what it would look like when he woke up in the morning.

"This isn't normal," Brigid said. "I mean, I don't react this way to people usually. Even when I haven't slept."

"Well, it's a problem we share, because I'm having at least as much trouble resisting you."

Chapter Four

Dane wanted to kiss Brigid again. And again, and again.

"That table is looking mighty fine," he said.

"We can't." She shook her head briskly. "I mean, I need to make dinner."

"You need a nap."

"I'll catch up on sleep later. I just have to figure out what's simple enough that I can make it safely and still impress Brendan."

"Let me help you." Dane let out a sigh when she cocked her head at him. "Apparently, my cooking is bad enough that he'll be impressed if you can get me to make something edible."

"It couldn't have been that bad," she said. "What were you going to make for dinner tonight?"

"Baked beans over boiled pasta."

Her eyes widened and her jaw dropped. "Baked beans over… No, no, no. You can't double up starches like that. I mean, not without adding some vegetables and a ton of fresh greens. But even then, with *baked* beans…"

She shivered.

"I guess it is that bad," he said.

It all tasted great to him. After a lifetime of nutrient bricks, what wouldn't? But the more he thought about it, the more he realized that Henry and Brendan's plates always had food left after meals. And Dane had caught them in the kitchen tons of times getting snacks or eating cereal.

"We'll keep the pasta idea," she said. "Spaghetti and meatballs. We'll have to use canned tomatoes, but I think we can make it work with what I've found in the cupboards so far."

"Sounds like a plan. I need to run downstairs for a few minutes, then I'll be back to help."

He reached up to take the bag of frozen peas from her and tossed it on the table. Before he could think better of it, he gripped the back of her neck and pulled her close for another kiss.

Bad idea.

Once he had a taste, he didn't want to stop. Her lips were impossibly soft, and this time, she was the one deepening the kiss. He grabbed her thigh, intent on getting her to straddle him again, when Barbara let out one of her high-pitched screeches.

Brigid broke the kiss, eyes wide and terrified as she pressed herself against Dane's chest and looked all around the room.

"What was that?" she said.

"Nothing for you to worry about."

"Are you kidding me? It sounded like it was coming from inside the house."

He sighed, not sure what to tell her. He still didn't want to lie to her, but doubted she'd take it very well if he confessed that there was a hormonally challenged Lyrian in the basement.

"That's just Barbara," he said.

"Barbara? Vay said that it was a mountain lion."

"Did she, now?" Dane chuckled. "Barbara's not a mountain lion."

"Then what is she?"

He opened his mouth, then closed it again and sighed.

Brigid rose from his lap and started pacing along the kitchen island. Her gaze kept roaming to the knives.

"She's not dangerous," he said. "At least, not to anybody but Zemanni."

"The helicopter pilot?"

Among other much more dangerous things.

"They have a history. Barbara doesn't like him. Just be nice to Henry and you'll be fine."

"This is crazy. You're really not going to tell me what she is."

"It's not for me to say. Brendan will have to be the one to tell you."

"This is about the NDA, isn't it?" Brigid said, still

pacing.

"NDA?"

"The one I had to sign to come work here. The one that says everything I see and hear in this place is classified. I can't even tell my family where I am." She paced faster, interlacing her fingers and pressing her palms together. "I mean, I know the drill with non-disclosure agreements. But I usually work for people in the entertainment industry. Producers, actors. I thought this was the site of a super-secret new film project they didn't want anybody to know about."

Dane stood and crossed over to her. He gripped her arms gently, making her pause and look up at him.

"Relax," he said. "It's going to be okay."

"Says the guy with a screeching howler-monkcy velociraptor in the basement."

He let out a chuckle. "Just don't let Barbara or Craig hear you talking like that."

"Craig? Wait a minute. One of those things was here earlier?"

"They're not *things*," he said.

"How am I supposed to know what to call them?"

Dane let out a sigh. This wasn't going well.

What the hell had Brendan been thinking, bringing an Earthling to the lodge? NDA or not, if Brigid told anybody what was really going on here…

No one would believe her.

It wasn't a very comforting thought, especially when he imagined the hardship it would cause her. He tried to think of something he could tell her that would reassure her without giving too much away.

"Barbara is my patient," Dane said. "She's...special. And she's pregnant."

"Pregnant?"

He nodded. "Yeah. She and Craig are going through a challenging time, and we're all trying to help them through it while getting our other work done."

"You make it sound like they're human. But no human could make a sound like that."

"What they are is family." Dane was surprised by his own vehemence—and by realizing that he meant it. "We can't tell you everything, but the work we're doing here is —"

"It's important." She scowled, glaring at him. "Brendan already told me."

"He wasn't lying." Dane searched for something—anything—he could tell her. He settled on the secrets that she could probably handle—the relatively mundane ones. "Brendan works for the government."

"And all I had to sign was an NDA? There has to be more to it than that. Security clearance, background checks —"

"And I'm sure Brendan's taken care of that all." Dane stepped a little closer, rubbing his thumbs over the soft skin of her arms. "You don't have to worry about the work we're doing. Apparently, we just need you to keep Brendan and Henry from starving. And Brendan wouldn't have hired you if he thought you couldn't handle it. If he didn't think you could help."

"I guess so. If it's that challenging of a pregnancy, it makes sense you need to be free to help her." Brigid took a deep breath, then blew it out. She stood straighter, squaring her shoulders. "Is she on a special diet? I can help with making food for her."

He smiled. How could he like someone so much so quickly?

"I appreciate the offer, but she's pretty happy with her peanuts." He nodded toward the pantry.

"That's all she eats? That can't be healthy."

Dane had no idea what was healthy for a pregnant Lyrian. He did know that what was healthy for everyone around her was giving her what she wanted.

"We can try her on some new foods when you're settled in, maybe," he said.

"My twin sister is a veterinarian. She's helped out tons of different kinds of animals and would be happy to help."

"Twin?" His heart seemed to stutter. "Like identical?"

"Yup, there are two of me." She laughed, then said, "Not really. Caitlin and I are really different. We can fool just about anybody into thinking we're the other sister, though. Usually, those kind of shenanigans are her idea."

Twins...

He thought of Marq, and about a million questions started lining up in his head. Questions that might raise Brigid's suspicions—or worse, someone else's.

If any of the other Sadirian soldiers found out Dane had a twin, that would bring up a whole different group of questions. Questions that could get him and Marq separated again—with mind-wipes to keep them that way.

Dane couldn't risk indulging his curiosity. He veered back to the original conversation.

"That's very kind of you to offer," he said. "But I think Henry and I will just have to stumble through this ourselves."

"Okay." She was quiet for a moment, then said, "This whole situation is really weird."

"Too weird?" He held his breath, hoping he hadn't scared her off with his honesty—such as it was.

After a moment, she shook her head. "Not too weird. But close."

"I can't really argue that point," he said. "Let me take some more boxes downstairs and check on Barbara. I'll be back soon."

"Okay. I'll get started on dinner."

As much as he wanted to, he didn't let himself lean in and kiss her this time. He'd learned his lesson.

Instead, he crossed to the pantry and picked up two boxes of peanuts, hefting them onto his shoulder. He couldn't wait to get back.

The rest of the house was quiet with everyone down in the basement. Dane hurried through the halls and down the concrete steps as quickly as he could without falling. Once he'd reached the lower level, he could hear voices from Craig and Barbara's chamber. He slowed as he approached the open door.

"It's a pair-bond," Barbara's voice rumbled down the halls. "I can smell it on every one of you that was in the room with them."

"They only just met," Henry said. "That seems a little fast."

"Didn't you know when you met me?" Vay asked.

"Well, that was…" Henry's voice faltered. "Okay, that's a good point. And it does seem like Earthlings and Sadirians bond really quickly. It still seems so improbable. I don't want Barbara to be disappointed if nothing comes of it. You know she's feeling sensitive."

"Sensitive?" Barbara boomed.

"Sensitive…to…pheromones," Henry said. "So, of course, she knows what she's talking about."

Dane could hear Barbara's loud exhalation. He figured he'd been lurking enough and headed through the doorway.

Barbara was buried in the nest of blankets and comforters she'd made by stripping every bed in the lodge early in the pregnancy. All that was visible of her enormous body was her blue-skinned face, surrounded by bristly white fur. She'd wrapped the blankets around her head so that even her batwing-like ears were hidden.

Henry and Vay were resting on cushions close by and Brendan stood in the corner, rearranging the boxes of peanuts. Everyone grew quiet, staring at Dane.

"What?" he said.

Brendan snickered. Dane glared at him.

Suddenly, a fur-covered arm was draped across Dane's shoulders. At the same time, the boxes of peanuts were lifted from his grasp.

"I think it's lovely that you're so taken with our new chef." Craig shimmered into view, his fur rippling as he dropped his natural camouflage.

"I was just trying to distract her so she didn't see you," Dane said.

Craig propped his one free hand on his hip. "Excuse me, I was cloaked."

"But the boxes weren't," Dane said. "How do you think she'd have reacted if she saw a bunch of boxes of peanuts just floating in the air?"

Craig snorted. He handed off the boxes of peanuts to Brendan, who was still smirking at Dane.

"Humans are more resilient than you think," Craig said. "Look at how well they've adapted to us."

He used his right arms to gesture toward Henry and Brendan, then squeezed Dane harder with the arm around his shoulder while ruffling his hair with his remaining free left hand.

How the heck do Lyrians keep track of all those arms?

"Quit it," Dane said.

Craig chuckled, then released Dane and returned to the nest with Barbara, sitting in front of her.

"How are you feeling, my sweet?" Craig said, a strange echoing coo sounding from deep in his chest. "Any better?"

"When did she not feel well?" Dane took a few steps forward, but everyone in front of him except Barbara quickly shook their heads to warn him off.

"Barbara picked up Zemanni's scent," Brendan said. "It was...upsetting."

"Upsetting?" Barbara said. "That scum tried to kill my family."

Her chest began making the popping sounds that preceded a screech. Henry and Vay covered their ears just in time before Barbara let loose with the loudest howl yet.

Dammit, Brigid is upstairs alone. That probably scared the crap out of her.

"That 'scum' is one of our allies now," Brendan said. "And a very powerful one."

Barbara's eyelids peeled back, revealing a disturbing amount of white around the blue oblong irises. "And I'm not?"

"Let's all stay calm," Henry said, reaching out to pat Barbara's shoulder.

Adopted nestling or not, Dane had to hand it to the

Earthling. There weren't many sentients in the galaxy that would have been brave enough to touch an irate, pregnant Lyrian. Even Craig was curling his head down submissively.

Dane had to intervene before he had even more patients. "I think a better term for Zemanni is 'useful'," Dane said. "I mean, there's no question who's more powerful. You tore him apart."

Barbara turned her gaze to Dane and his heart began to pound. Taking the target off the others didn't mean he wanted it on himself.

"I wasn't thorough enough," Barbara said. "He put himself back together."

Crap.

She started making that popping noise again. At this rate, Brigid would run away by the time Dane returned upstairs. She might think the woods were less frightening. He almost agreed at the moment.

"That just means he's reusable," Dane said, using his most placating tone. "If the *Reckoning* shows up with their gunports firing, we can toss them Zemanni to buy us some time."

Craig chuckled.

"We aren't using Zemanni as cannon fodder," Brendan said.

"It was just a suggestion." Dane shrugged, watching for Barbara's reaction surreptitiously. He relaxed a bit as her eyes returned to normal and she settled back among her blankets.

"'Cannon fodder'." Barbara chuckled from deep in her nest.

"If everybody's okay down here, I need to get back upstairs," Dane said.

Every single person in the room grinned at him. Only Brendan had the decency to half-try to hide it.

Dammit.

"To make dinner," Dane added.

That killed their smiles. The Earthlings', anyway.

"I thought that Brigid was going to be cooking from now on." Henry shifted around as if trying to get comfortable in the blankets and pillows he was sitting on.

"Relax," Dane said. "She's going to teach me how to cook."

Henry didn't look reassured. He glanced over at Brendan, and said, "That's…nice."

"We're just doing spaghetti and meatballs tonight," Dane said.

"Meatballs?" Henry's face paled.

"You know, you could have told me you didn't like my cooking," Dane said.

"Who didn't like it?" Vay glanced at Henry and Brendan, both of whom were staring at the ceiling. "You didn't? But it has so much flavor."

Henry took Vay's hand and kissed it. "Yes, but the flavor

isn't usually tuna salad with fish from a can and marshmallow cream as the binder."

"And pickle relish," Brendan said.

Henry barely suppressed a gagging sound. "Please. Don't remind me about the relish."

"I like Dane's tuna sandwiches." Vay smiled at Dane.

"Sweetie, you've eaten nutrient bricks your whole life," Henry said. "You sprinkle fruitcake in your cereal."

Brendan stepped forward. "I think what we're trying to say is that Dane has more important things to focus on than feeding us. Like studying Barbara's physiology and making sure her pregnancy is progressing well."

"My pregnancy is progressing perfectly." Barbara reached for Craig, who quickly wrapped his arms around her. "It's almost time to pass the new nestling to my mate."

"Wait, what?" Dane said. "You didn't tell me the male had a part in gestation."

"I'm *primarily* male." Craig let out a huff of breath through his nostrils. "Expand your thinking beyond binary genders."

Damn, there was a lot Dane needed to learn. He was completely out of his depth with Barbara's pregnancy.

Lyrians were so secretive about their physiology—with good reason, since sentients like Zemanni hunted them for their camouflaging pelts.

"You know, that's the kind of thing your doctor really should know," Dane said.

"I don't need a doctor," Barbara growled. "I just need my family close."

"Let's give them some space." Brendan crossed to Dane and put a hand on his shoulder. "Henry can try to find out if there's anything else we might need to know about."

"I'd appreciate that." Dane nodded in Henry's direction, then let Brendan nudge him out the door.

Chapter Five

This was the lamest first meal Brigid had ever cooked for a client. She was having trouble caring, after seeing the delight on Dane's face while they were making it.

He hung on every word, his brow knit in concentration as he asked questions and really thought through what she was saying. She'd never taught someone with such a drive to learn.

"Why six places?" she asked, putting the last fork next to the place settings. "There are only four people here now."

Unless Craig or Barbara was joining them. Brigid shuddered at the thought.

She still didn't know what she had gotten herself into. Wild animals were living in the basement, and she had no clue what they even were.

"Aren't you joining us?" Dane asked.

"I don't usually eat with my clients. The kitchen table is fine."

Her cheeks tingled as she remembered what she and

Dane had almost done on that table. Cooking with him had gone a long way in soothing her frayed nerves, especially after hearing another of those howls.

Dane shook his head. "Brendan won't be okay with that. Honestly, none of us will be."

She didn't know how to respond. She was already so far out of her normal routines.

This wasn't going to be like any of her other jobs. She'd started to wonder about it the moment she saw Zemanni land in that fancy helicopter. The feeling had only become stronger when she met Dane.

"What about the sixth place?"

"Brendan always sets a place for his wife, Kira," Dane said.

Well… That was pretty sweet. And comparatively normal.

"Where is she?"

"She's at our new facility in Florida."

"Overseeing the construction?"

Dane shook his head. "Training, mostly."

"Training in what?"

He turned to her, his eyes wider than usual and his mouth slightly open. It was the same deer-in-headlights expression he'd had earlier when she was heading into topics he couldn't talk about.

"You could tell me, but then you'd have to kill me?" She laughed.

Dane looked stricken. "I'd never let that happen."

"It was just a joke."

A joke that he'd taken seriously.

"Wait, that's not… That's not a possibility, is it?" she said.

Before Dane could respond, Vay walked in, followed by a tall, lanky man. He was thin and pale, with tousled brown hair and the beginnings of a beard. His rumpled clothes and the dark circles under his eyes made Brigid wonder when he'd last been able to get a good night's sleep.

His companion was just as energetic as when Brigid had met her, though. Vay had a tight hold on Henry's hand, leading him to the table, and her smile lit up the room. Brigid found herself smiling back.

"I'm so excited to try spaghetti." Vay sat with Henry on the far side of the table. "Do your meatballs have ketchup and cherry sauce, too?"

"Cherry sauce?" Brigid said.

"Don't ask." Dane came up behind her from the archway that led to the kitchen, holding a huge bowl of noodles. "I was just…trying something."

"There's no cherry sauce," Brigid said. "Or ketchup."

"Oh." Vay's smile faded.

How could she be disappointed at no ketchup and cherry sauce with spaghetti and meatballs? Brigid suppressed a shudder, hoping that those three things had at least not been served all together.

"I think you'll like what Dane and I have cooked up, though," Brigid said.

Vay smiled again, but it was more subdued. "I'm sure we'll love it. Right, Henry?" She leaned against Henry's arm.

"Hmm, what?" He gazed around the room, his eyes a bit unfocused. "Yes. It smells great, actually."

"Next time, we'll make garlic bread to go with it," Brigid said.

She moved to one of the chairs opposite Henry and Vay, but Dane caught her by the elbow.

"That's Kira's seat," he said.

"Oh, sorry." Brigid looked around. "Where should I sit?"

"Here's fine." He gestured to one of the heads of the table.

That just didn't seem right, but at least she'd have a good view of everyone and could gauge their reactions. Dane sat next to her as she lowered herself into her seat.

"Sorry I'm late." Brendan rushed into the room, sitting across from her at the opposite end of the table. He smiled as he took in the dishes before him and said, "This looks great."

"Dane was a big help," Brigid said.

Henry had picked up some salad with the tongs, but froze. He stared at the leaves as if inspecting them carefully.

"It's fine, really," she said.

"My cooking couldn't have been that bad," Dane said.

Henry stammered. "No... Sure... I mean..."

"We really appreciate everything you've done," Brendan said. "And I'm glad you're still taking an interest."

"You did a great job." Brigid reached over and squeezed Dane's hand.

The moment their skin touched, she felt more of that white-hot electricity coursing through her nerves. She'd never experienced chemistry like this before. The way his pupils widened as he stared at her, gripping her fingers before she had a chance to pull away, she was pretty sure he felt it, too.

"Careful, Vay," Henry said.

Vay was holding a container of red pepper flakes that Brigid had put on the table for those who liked to kick up the heat in their meal.

"Of what?" Vay said. "These are so pretty and colorful."

Pretty?

Brigid had never heard them described that way.

"They're hot," Henry said.

Vay looked at the glass canister, then held it in both hands, a thoughtful expression on her face. "I don't think so. The jar is cool."

"No, the flakes are hot." Henry let out a frustrated breath. "It's a different kind of heat."

"It's just to add some spice," Brigid said. "You don't

need to use it."

Vay's face brightened. "I like spice. Salt and sugar are my favorites."

"Sugar's not really..." Henry's voice trailed off.

Vay must have never had spicy food before. Henry seemed to be struggling with how to explain it. Brigid decided to help him out. She was the chef, after all.

"There's a substance in those called capsaicin that causes a chemical reaction with the heat sensors in your mouth," Brigid said. "If you put too much of that on your food, it'll feel like you're being burned."

"Wow." Vay sprinkled a few flakes into her palm, then set down the shaker and carefully picked up a flake and put it on her tongue.

At least that one's an adventurous eater.

Vay's eyes widened and she smiled. "It does!" she said. Her face scrunched up and she stuck out her tongue, wiping it with her hand. "Ow, ow, ow."

"I can get you some milk." Henry started to stand, but Vay stopped him.

"No, it's okay," she said. "It's passing now." She turned to Brigid, beaming. "That was amazing!"

Brigid could barely believe it. She had achieved a bit of fame in her circles for her use of science in cuisine, and this group was impressed by the capsaicin reaction of a single red pepper flake.

She was totally making a baking soda volcano later.

They wouldn't be able to eat it, but it would probably knock their socks off to see just what kitchen ingredients could do.

"I think Kira's ready to join us," Brendan said, looking up from the fancy silver watch he wore.

Brigid glanced around the room. "I thought she was in Florida."

"She is." Brendan smiled enigmatically. "But there are ways around that, with the right technology."

"Just remember that NDA," Vay said, smiling toward Brigid.

Light flickered in Kira's empty chair, expanding into the shape of a woman. Her form was silvered and transparent, like a hologram in a sci-fi movie.

Brigid's skin prickled in goosebumps. That was so cool! But she couldn't tell anyone about it. Suddenly, the NDA made a lot more sense.

First the high-tech helicopter, and now this? Brigid pressed her lips together, biting them to keep them shut tight. So many questions were pushing to get out, none of which she would probably get answers for.

They could tell me, but then they'd have to kill me.

The thought helped curb her curiosity. Instead of focusing on her questions, Brigid looked at Kira. The image of Kira, anyway. Brendan's wife had long, dark hair, strong features, and was absolutely, drop-dead gorgeous.

What is it about the women here?

The guys were cute, in a nerdy kind of way. Well, except for Dane, who was as Hollywood hot as Kira and Vay. For a moment, Brigid wondered if this was some kind of movie set after all. But she'd been on movie sets before, and had never seen anything like the level of technology that everyone around the table seemed to take in stride.

"Hello," Brendan said.

Brigid had never heard a single word hold so much emotion. The expression on Brendan's face as he looked at Kira made Brigid's heart beat faster and her stomach warm. There was so much love and longing in his gaze.

She wondered if anyone would ever look at her that way. Her gaze flicked to Dane before she could stop herself. He was still looking at her, holding her hand, his thumb lightly brushing across her knuckles.

"Greetings." Kira's voice was strong and richer than most women's. From the way Brendan smirked, Brigid wondered if the pair was sharing some inside joke.

"Sarah said you made a special request for our meals to match today," Kira said. Her plate held a transparent version of salad and spaghetti that looked very similar to what was already on Vay and Henry's plates.

"It's something of a special occasion," Brendan said. "We're celebrating our new chef."

"New chef?" Kira looked around the table, her stern gaze finally settling on Brigid as if they were in the same room.

Could Kira be sitting at a table with holographic versions of everyone at the lodge? Brigid did her best not to look around the room for cameras. Instead, she lifted her hand and waved.

"Hi," Brigid said.

Kira's lips pulled into a tight line. She turned back to Brendan. "Do you really think this is a good idea after what happened with the last one?"

The last one?

"She's already fitting in nicely." Brendan briefly glanced at Dane.

"How long has she been here?" Kira asked.

"A couple of hours," Brendan said.

"Um, excuse me." Brigid raised the hand Dane wasn't holding onto. "What happened to the last chef?"

Everybody at the table turned to stare at her. Dane squeezed her hand tighter.

"He couldn't handle the noises Barbara made," Dane said. "In the early days of her pregnancy, she was a lot more vocal."

"*More* vocal?" Brigid shuddered. She couldn't imagine hearing that noise more often she already had.

Kira slowly turned toward Brendan. "She knows about Barbara?"

"I don't," Brigid broke in quickly. "I mean, all I know is that she loves eating peanuts and lives in the basement with Craig and that they're not howler-monkey velociraptor hybrids."

Henry had been taking a drink, and he choked on it. He quickly covered his mouth with his napkin as he tried to stop his coughing. Vay patted his back.

"Could you please try not to drown at the table?" Dane said.

Henry gave him a thumb's up.

"That's all?" Kira raised an eyebrow, her voice dripping with sarcasm. She turned back to Brendan.

He took a deep breath and slowly let it out. Smiling at her, he lifted his hand. Brigid saw a flash of silver from a wide metal wristband he was wearing under his sweater sleeve.

Kira stared at his palm for a moment before resting her hand above his. Bright motes of light sparked where their skin should connect.

Whoa...

"I need to be here," Brendan said. "And you need to be there. This is what we have right now. But I also need to feel that you're with me. Everyday comforts are important."

"Brendan..." Kira reached out to him, her hand hovering just above his cheek. Brendan closed his eyes and lifted his hand to hers. More of those little motes of light sparked where their hands would be touching.

What the heck kind of technology was this? The hairs on the back of Brigid's neck stood on end and she gripped

Dane's hand harder.

There was so much going on beneath the surface of "cooking for an eccentric billionaire." And the surface was pretty weird to begin with.

Whatever she'd landed herself into, the way Brendan and Kira were looking at each other hit Brigid hard. That kind of love was something she dreamed of finding. It was something worth fighting for and protecting, even if she wasn't the one actively experiencing it.

It sure as heck was worth putting up with a yowly whatever-it-was in the basement. If Brigid could give them some comfort while they were separated by cooking for Brendan and giving him a sense of normalcy, she'd do it.

"I'm not learning as quickly as I should," Kira said.

Brendan opened his eyes and smiled at her. "You're doing your best. You'll get it in time."

"We don't have time to—" Kira turned toward Brigid, her mouth snapping shut.

"I can go," Brigid said. "It sounds like you have some things to talk about."

Brendan shook his head. "It's okay. There are lots of other topics that are better for the table. Like Dane's cooking lessons."

"These meatballs are amazing." Vay's mouth was so full, Brigid could hardly understand her. "Cygnus X."

Wait, what did she say?

Vay started sawing at her spaghetti noodles, cheeks

puffed up like a chipmunk. "I can't wait to try the spaghetti."

"That's actually not how you're supposed to eat it," Brigid said.

Vay's eyes widened as she looked at her. She swallowed, then said, "Oh no. Did I break some cultural protocol?"

"Cultural protocol?" Brigid laughed. "I guess that's what this is. Here, let me show you."

Brigid finally pulled her hand away from Dane's, then picked up the big spoon at her place setting. She scooped up a few noodles with her fork and put the tines on the spoon, using it to keep the noodles in place as she twirled the fork, wrapping the noodles around the tines. As she did, Vay's eyes—and smile—grew bigger.

"That looks like so much fun." Vay picked up her spoon and mimicked Brigid's actions perfectly.

"Wow, you're a natural," Brigid said.

Dane had been about to bite into a meatball, but he flinched. The movement knocked it from his fork. It hit the table with a splat, then rolled off the edge and onto the floor.

"Shit," Dane said.

"I've got it." Brigid used her napkin to quickly wipe the tomato sauce from the table, then ducked under it to clean up the floor. "It's just like that kid's song… We should grate some fresh cheese next time."

Her voice trailed off as she sat back up and saw that

everyone was staring at her.

"What does it mean to be a natural?" Vay said, her expression oddly guarded.

Henry jumped in. "I think she just meant it usually takes people longer to figure out how to do that so well."

"Oh," Vay said. She took another bite of meatball, staring at her plate intently.

After a few moments of everyone eating in silence, Brigid said, "I kind of feel like *I've* broken some cultural protocols."

Vay let out a little laugh and smiled at her.

"I know there are things—lots of things—you can't tell me," Brigid said. "And the longer I'm here, the more I'm understanding that. But if there are things I should—and can—know about you all, I'd like to learn them. This is already unlike any job I've had before, and I don't want to step on anybody's toes."

"You're really tiny," Vay said.

Brigid felt her eyebrows lift. Sure, she was short and Vay was supermodel tall, but that was a weird thing to say. Then again, what about this job *wasn't* weird?

"I don't know whether to say 'thanks' or 'hey!'" Brigid said, forcing a smile.

Vay was back to stuffing meatballs into her mouth. She somehow managed, "I just meant it wouldn't hurt if you stepped on anybody's toes. Unless you stomped on them. But you don't seem like the type to do that."

"I'm not," Brigid said. "I mean, I wouldn't."

Vay smiled, her cheeks huge. Brigid fought the urge to laugh at the comical expression, and settled for smiling back instead.

Weirdest job ever.

But she was kind of starting to like it.

Chapter Six

Dane put the last dish in the dishwasher just as Brigid entered the kitchen. Her dark hair was wet and combed back from her face and she was wearing flannel pajamas and fluffy pink slippers shaped like some sort of animal with long, floppy ears.

She stared at the dishwasher for a moment. "This is really going to take some getting used to."

"Given everything you've seen and heard today, I'm not sure what you're talking about."

She smiled as she approached. "Normally, when I'm hired to do a job, I'm treated at best like an employee and at worst like a servant. Often a not-very-appreciated servant. Everyone here is being so nice."

"And that's a problem?" He started up the dishwasher.

"I guess not. It's just strange."

"Well, in case you haven't noticed, we're a strange lot."

She laughed. "Yeah, I did kind of notice that."

He walked a little closer. He wanted to wrap his arms around her, to kiss her and maybe carry her upstairs to one of their rooms. Instead, he leaned against the short side of the kitchen island counter, trying to feign a sense of ease.

"Did your shower help?" he asked.

"I feel a lot better now. I think I've caught a second wind." She grinned, and added, "That means I have a renewed burst of energy."

"I'm pretty good with idioms."

"Vay is adorable when she can't figure one out. She freaked when I told her I needed to take a shower 'to feel human again' and gave me a big hug even after I explained it."

Dane laughed. "Yeah, I can see her doing that. What else do you need?"

Brigid shook her head. "See, that's just what I'm talking about. I'm supposed to be seeing to all of your needs."

"We need you to be happy here."

"Mission accomplished."

"I'm glad to hear it."

Her cheeks turned pink as she stared at him for a few moments before looking away.

"About earlier..." They both spoke at the same time. Same words, same tone, and then laughed together. That had never happened to him before.

He straightened, stepping closer. "About earlier," he said.

"Yeah..."

The skin on his arms prickled into goosebumps as he

fought the urge to reach out to her. If he touched her, he wasn't sure what would happen.

He'd cleared off the counter. But then, if Brendan didn't want them doing anything on the table, he probably wouldn't like anything happening on the counter, either.

"Do you want to watch a movie, maybe?" Brigid said. "I know I should be exhausted, but I'm too wired to sleep just yet."

"A movie sounds great."

The entertainment room was seldom used, close by, and had an overstuffed couch with plenty of room for them to... get comfortable.

Her smile grew. "I'll make popcorn."

Popcorn?

She started going through the cabinets, looking for whatever popcorn was. He would offer to help, but didn't have a clue what she was looking for.

After all the strange topics that had come up during and after dinner, he didn't want to give her more things to wonder about. Their ignorance of everyday Earthling things had caused Brigid to lift an eyebrow more than once.

She was handling everything so well—unlike the previous chef, who had seen a box of floating peanuts one too many times and become convinced the place was haunted.

At least he'd been focused on ghosts and never once mentioned anything about aliens. Dane doubted the guy would cause any problems for them with the huge payment Brendan had given him when he left.

Dane still wished that the others had told him he wasn't doing a good enough job when he'd stepped in to fill that void. Then again, if he had tried harder, Brendan wouldn't have felt the need to hire Brigid.

Dane had met countless other sentients, including quite a few Earthlings. He'd never reacted to anyone like he did to Brigid.

"Aha." She pulled out a small box, then opened it up. Inside, there were several folded bags wrapped in plastic.

She tore open the plastic and unfolded the bag, then set it inside the microwave. "Can you get us out a bowl?"

"Sure." He reached over her to open the cabinet that held the dishes Brendan and Henry used to eat cereal.

"Not that kind of bowl." She shook her head and laughed. "Bigger."

How the heck was that tiny flat bag going to produce something that needed a bigger bowl?

He closed the door as she punched in numbers on the microwave. The process reminded him of how nutrient bricks were created and deployed back on the *Arbiter*.

A chill threaded down his spine at the thought of his ship—and the one just like it that was on the way.

The *Reckoning* could reach Earth in a matter of weeks. Even with the Vegans offering to use their advanced technology to assist in defending Earth, there was every chance of violence. Dane had high stakes on both sides.

Dane's thoughts had been swirling around the *Reckoning's* crew ever since Brigid made that comment about Vay being 'a natural'. Specifically, he kept thinking about the second-in-command, Marq.

Dane's brother.

Dane's not-genetically engineered brother.

The Coalition might get their ass kicked by the Vegans when they arrived at Earth, but Marq and Dane were still soldiers. If anyone found out that they knew about each other, they'd get mind-wipes and be reassigned far enough apart that they'd never have a chance to reconnect, just like what had been done to their parents. It was a miracle Dane and Marq had discovered each other in the first place—and the truth about themselves.

There was just too much to unpack when it came to Marq. How the hell could Dane keep his brother safe—and protect their secret—when the *Reckoning* arrived?

If he kept thinking about it, he'd lose even more sleep. At this rate, he'd be completely non-functional when it was time to head to the Florida base to take their stand.

Besides, he had much more pleasant things to occupy his attention—like Brigid.

Bigger bowls were in the cabinet in the kitchen island. He was just turning to fetch one when he heard the first burst of weapon fire.

"Get down," he yelled.

She let out a yelp as he grabbed her by the waist and pulled her against his chest. Ducking low, he spun them away from the sound. It was coming from right where Brigid had been standing, and increasing in frequency.

He half-dragged her to the other side of the kitchen island, then pushed her to the ground, covering her with his body while he tried to make sense of where the attack was coming from.

"What are you doing?" Brigid yelled.

"Saving you from whatever that is," he said.

"That's the popcorn!"

"What?" He scanned the room, but didn't see any movement.

"Dane, look at me." Brigid put her hands on his cheeks and tugged till he complied. "That is the sound popcorn makes when you cook it. That's why it's called *pop*corn."

The noise was dying down, with only intermittent bursts of sound. His heart was pounding and his mouth had gone dry.

"How the hell can food make so much noise?" he said.

"The water in the corn is heated to a temperature that causes steam to build up in it. The starches in the kernel expand as it pops, and then they set pretty much instantly, resulting in popcorn."

"What?"

"It's just food," she said. "You're safe. I'm safe. Everyone's safe."

"Well then, I guess this is…"

Yet more completely unreasonable and suspicious behavior.

He kept that thought to himself, and instead said, "This is really overreacting."

Brigid laughed. "Maybe a little bit. Have you really never had popcorn before?"

"Never heard of it before today."

"That is insane. Where are you even from?" Her expression fell as she hurried to reassure him. "I mean, you don't have to tell me. I don't need to know."

He wished he could tell her, but that really would be insane. She'd probably freak out if she knew he was an alien. Especially after what they'd almost done earlier in the day.

Dammit.

He couldn't let anything happen between them without her knowing what he was. He couldn't believe that hadn't occurred to him already. And here he was, lying on top of her, their bodies pressed together.

Her hair was fanned out around her head, her blue eyes shining up at him. The pink cast to her cheeks had deepened and she was staring at his lips. She was breathing fast, her breasts tight against his chest.

Every cell in his body told him to stay—to kiss her, to shift his weight just a little so he could feel her heat. His dick pulsed at the thought, sending a shudder through him.

This couldn't happen, though. It would never happen, because he couldn't tell her about who and what he was.

He sat back on his heels, knees on either side of her body, and blew out a breath.

"So, um…" she said. "Movie?"

He laughed and shook his head. "Yeah."

Chapter Seven

The only reason Brigid was sure she wasn't having some sort of really vivid dream was that she and Dane weren't having sex back on the kitchen floor. Her subconscious would never be that mean to her.

Instead, they were sitting on opposite ends of a comfortable couch in front of a TV screen that took up an entire wall. A huge wall.

She didn't understand why Dane was staying so far away from her. Things had been hot and heavy with them up to now, and the sudden change in his behavior was getting to her more than she wanted to admit.

She barely knew the guy. They'd only just met. What did she care if he didn't want to hold hands or put his arm around her or do…other things while the movie played?

Of course, he could not know movie first-date etiquette. He didn't even know what popcorn was, for crying out loud. The bowl sat on the coffee table in front of them, perfuming the air with that delicious scent so unique to the traditional treat.

"What do you want to watch?" she asked.

"Anything, really." He pointed the remote at the screen and started pressing buttons. "Brendan has it all."

"How about something sci-fi?"

He turned toward her. "Sci-fi?"

"Yeah. Girls can like sci-fi, you know."

"I never thought otherwise."

"Are you not into it? Because we could watch something else."

"No, that's… That's fine. Anything in particular?"

Something maybe a little scary. But not too scary. She was still hoping to bridge the gap that had suddenly appeared between them. At the same time, after the weird day she'd had, she didn't want to freak herself out—or Dane.

"How about, *Invasion of the Body Snatchers*?" she said. "Either version."

"O…kay. I'll see what I can do." He started scrolling through titles on the screen.

"Wow, Brendan really does have a huge collection," she murmured. "I'll get the lights."

She hopped up and headed to the switch. The room was bathed in a soft white glow as she turned the main lights off.

Dane's reaction to the popcorn had raised even more questions. Brendan worked for the government, she knew. And with how Dane had grabbed her and thrown her to the ground, she was sure he'd seen active duty.

For all she knew, he still *was* on active duty, protecting Brendan and the others while they worked on their secret projects. She still didn't understand how they could have managed to hire a civilian chef, though.

What she *did* know was that they all seemed like kind and genuine people, if a little weird. Okay, a lot weird. But they were treating her better than any place she'd ever worked—and that was in addition to the ridiculous salary she was making.

Then there was Dane.

She'd never been so drawn to someone. The chemistry they had going on was nuclear. She wanted more of that. More of his kisses. More of his touch.

She would settle for sitting a little closer when she returned to the couch. Her plans were thwarted, though—he had moved the bowl of popcorn onto the cushions beside him.

She sat on the other side of it, hoping that the darkness of the room would hide her disappointment.

What had she done to turn him off so suddenly and completely? When he'd been straddling her in the kitchen, his desire had been impressively apparent. She knew he wanted her just as much as she wanted him.

The movie started up. She looked over at him, but he was focused on the screen.

"Let me know if you get scared," she said.

He let out a little laugh and shook his head. "I don't see that happening, but sure."

"Thanks for keeping me company while I wind down."

"Sure."

Even her attempts to reconnect via conversation were falling flat. She retreated into her thoughts as the movie played in the background, her mind wandering through all the different things they'd said and done, searching for anything that might explain his behavior. Nothing made sense.

A sharp intake of breath brought her back to the room some time later. She glanced over at Dane, who was staring wide-eyed at the screen.

She looked at it, too, trying to determine what was freaking him out. He'd picked the 1950's version, and between the black-and-white film and lack of special effects, it didn't seem like it could scare anybody.

"Are you okay?" she asked.

"What? No. I mean yeah. Why wouldn't I be?"

"You look a little upset."

"This movie is…" He shook his head. "It's profoundly disturbing."

She laughed before she could help herself. "Really? I mean, I guess the concepts might be."

"You go to sleep and you wake up somebody else." His voice grew harsher as he continued. "Your body, your mind, your memory, your thoughts—none of it truly yours.

Everything is gone and rewritten, and you don't even know it. Emotions stripped." He picked up the remote and stopped the movie, then threw the remote down on the coffee table.

"Dane…"

He crushed his palms against his eyes, shaking his head. "Who the hell came up with this? Who could have known?"

"Known what?"

She moved the empty popcorn bowl to the coffee table, then knelt next to him on the couch. Cautiously, she reached out to him. When he didn't pull away, she shifted closer.

"I'm really sorry," she said. "This is just a movie I used to watch with my family. We would joke about pod people and alien invasions and—"

Dane dropped his hands and glared at her.

"I'm sorry, I just…" Her voice trailed off. She had no idea what to say, especially since she had no idea why he was freaking out again.

How the heck could pod people upset him so much? This was even worse than the popcorn.

Maybe he's part of an alien invasion and is worried you're going to figure it out after watching this show.

Her sleep-deprived brain wasn't being helpful.

Then again, it was pretty strange that he didn't know what popcorn was. Or baseball. Or how to use an ice pack, especially as a doctor.

A dozen little things from their conversations and interactions paraded themselves in front of her mind—things she'd dismissed as him "not being from around here." It sure seemed strange he couldn't tell her where he was from.

In the background, her brain kept reminding her of Craig and Barbara—the not-howler monkey velociraptor hybrids living in the basement and only eating peanuts. Oh right, and Barbara was pregnant, so there would be more of them soon.

Maybe Dane wasn't part of an alien invasion, but he and the others could be working to stop one. That would explain the high tech gadgetry and—

Oh my God. I need to sleep.

She also needed to give Dane some space. Or a hug. Or kiss him.

"I don't know why this is upsetting you," she said.

"I just need to sort some stuff out." He stood and walked over to the screen, one hand in the back pocket of his jeans and the other holding his hair away from his face.

"Okay, I can just…" She looked around, searching for some way she could help. Her gaze landed on the empty popcorn bowl. There weren't even any unpopped kernels in the bottom.

She must have been really deep in thought to not notice him eating all that. And he must have loved it.

"I'll make us some more popcorn," she said.

"I don't want more popcorn."

A booming voice sounded from behind the couch. "I do."

Brigid saw Dane's eyes widen and his mouth drop open, almost like it was in slow motion. He started forward as she turned her head.

Her brain shut down. It just...stopped processing. Because what she was seeing was absolutely impossible.

From her elevated position sitting on her knees on the couch, she could easily see the floor space between her and the door. The *large* floor space that was completely taken up by a giant, white-furred, blue-faced *thing*.

It was as big as a rhinoceros, but shaped like a gorilla. Sort of.

The arms were different.

There were four of them.

Blue batwing-shaped ears twitched on either side of its head, and its pupils were elongated sideways like a goat's. As Brigid stared, it smiled at her, revealing rows and rows of jagged teeth, like in a shark's mouth.

"Oh my freaking God, what are you?" The words poured out so quickly, they slurred together. Brigid's voice rose in pitch with each syllable.

The thing on the floor cocked its head at her. "I'm Barbara."

Chapter Eight

Brigid sucked in a breath, her chest expanding. Just before she let out a scream, Dane managed to clamp a hand over her mouth. He wrapped his arm around her stomach, crushing her against his chest.

"Shh," he hissed, his lips close against her ear. "Barbara's not going to hurt you, but she's extra-sensitive right now and tends to break things when she's upset."

The scream he was stifling turned into a high-pitched "Eeeeeee!"

Dammit, how had this happened?

"Barbara is a Lyrian," he said.

Barbara snorted. "Like that explains anything."

She had a point.

"She and her baby need to be protected," Dane said. "They're extremely rare life forms."

"From the Lyra system," Barbara added. "Hence 'Lyrian'."

"That's not helping!" Dane said.

Barbara shook her head. "Fine, I'll help. My mate,

Craig, and I have been visiting Earth for hundreds of solar cycles—I guess I should say years. Your cryptozoologists usually call us Bigfoot, though we prefer space-Sasquatch, since our little Henry is so fond of describing us that way. Henry lost his parents in a car crash not terribly long ago, and even though he's considered grown for your species, we adopted him anyway."

Brigid stopped making the sustained "eee" sound, and her breathing began to slow. Dane could feel her relaxing as he was tensing up. Brigid shouldn't know any of this. After seeing Barbara, though… It was a little late to try to hide the truth.

"Craig wanted to give Henry a sibling, which I knew was a bad idea, with the *Reckoning* on the way." Barbara leaned forward, and said, "That's a warship sent by the Coalition of Planets to investigate the 'unauthorized influence Earth is having on their soldiers'—meaning, they plan to arrest or reassign everyone and give mind-wipes to the Earthlings involved."

Brigid stiffened again.

"But don't worry," Barbara said. "We have the Vegans on our side. Most of the Earthlings call them 'little lizard people from the Vega system.' It's pronounced 'vayguns', but apparently, you have a group of people who call themselves vegans, which is great for you, because it led to a misunderstanding that has them claiming Earth as their new homeworld. Not the Earthling-vegans but the Vega-

Vegans."

Dane had never heard Barbara talk this much. What the hell had gotten into her?

"The *Reckoning* doesn't stand a chance against the Vegans." Barbara looked thoughtful for a moment, then said, "Well, unless that new mysterious technology that's surfaced lately is more advanced than we thought."

"Barbara," Dane warned.

"You really do have a strange effect on Sadirians." Barbara went on as if he hadn't spoken. "And they seem to do the same to you. All of these flash-fire pair-bonds have been so inspiring. The pheromones you're both putting off right now is exactly the kind of thing that prompted Craig and I to make a nestling earlier than we intended. Well, except for the fear response that's gotten mixed in."

Brigid said something, but the words were muffled. Dane slowly removed his hand.

"Pheromones?" Brigid said.

"Earthlings and Sadirians are biologically compatible." Barbara let out a little laugh. "Some couples more than others. And your bodies put off chemicals signaling that."

"How..." Brigid leaned closer to Dane, pressing herself more firmly against his chest. Her voice was shaking. "Why..."

"Oh, I hope for your future nestlings' sake that this is just the shock making you stupid," Barbara said.

"Hey!" Dane and Brigid said the word at the same time.

Barbara spoke slowly as she explained. "The intense physical attraction you feel for each other is causing your bodies to secrete arousal chemicals that I can detect."

"I get that," Brigid said.

She sounded more angry than afraid. That was an improvement. Probably.

"Wait a minute." Brigid twisted around in his arms, staring up at him with wide eyes. "Does that mean that you're an alien, too?"

It was way too late to try to lie to her. Before he could respond, Barbara jumped in again, using that same patronizing tone.

"Yes, he is an alien from outer space," Barbara said. "Sadr-4 specifically. That's in the Gamma Cygni system. And I'm from the Lyra system. That's why they call me Lyrian. And you're from Earth."

"I know where I'm from," Brigid snapped.

Barbara grinned. Dane started to wonder if Barbara was doing this on purpose—antagonizing Brigid to snap her out of being afraid. He didn't know many people who were familiar with Lyrians who would yell at them like that, let alone a sentient who was seeing one for the first time.

"Now that we have that all settled," Dane nodded toward Barbara, "can we please discuss why you're here?"

"I live here," Barbara said.

Dane let out a sigh. "Yeah, and your nest is in the basement. You said you'd stay in your nest until…"

His stomach clenched and his skin felt electrified. Barbara's eyes widened as they stared at each other.

At the same time, they said, "Until the nestling was ready to emerge."

Dane released Brigid and ran to Barbara. He reached for the center of her chest, where he knew the nestling was, but she swatted him away. Brigid was at his side. She'd come closer, too.

Could she be trying to help? The situation had to be terrifying her.

"Don't confuse it," Barbara yelled. "You do not want it trying to attach to you instead of Craig."

"Shit," Dane said. "What do I do?"

"How do you not know what to do?" Brigid said. "Aren't you a doctor?"

"I'm a *Sadirian* doctor," Dane yelled. "We don't have babies."

"Don't have…" Brigid shook her head. "Then where do Sadirians come from?"

"They're genetically engineered and grown to adulthood in maturation chambers," Barbara said.

"You can't be serious." Brigid actually laughed. When neither joined in, she said, "Oh my God. You can't be serious!"

Dane slapped his hand on his watch, activating the comm channel. "Sitewide alert. The nestling is coming. We need Craig in the movie room now."

A split-second later, he heard a crash from the basement. The floor shook and a pounding sound vibrated through the room.

"Craig's on his way." Henry's voice sounded over the comm. "What's Barbara doing in the movie room?"

"I was hungry for something different," Barbara said.

Brigid shook her head. "She must have smelled the popcorn."

"Was that..." Henry began. "Was that Brigid?"

"Yeah," Dane said. "But we have bigger problems."

Craig burst into the room. Amazingly, Brigid only let out a little 'eep'.

"Barbara." Craig rushed to his mate and wrapped all four of his arms around her. "Is it really time?"

"I think so," she said.

"But it's early." The worry in Craig's voice was clear.

Barbara just chuckled. "Earth food is incredibly nourishing. He wouldn't be ready to emerge this soon otherwise."

"He?" Craig said.

"Sounds like you're getting a baby brother." Dane fought back the emotion that surged in him.

Henry was going to get a chance to know his brother—even if they were two totally different species. Dane wished he had been able to do the same with Marq.

Craig looked over his shoulder at them and smiled. "You should probably leave now."

"Right," Brigid said. "This is private."

"Sure," Craig said. "That's why."

A long, thin tentacle whipped out from Barbara's chest. Craig caught it quickly, and said, "Somebody's eager for a change of body chemistry."

He ran one of his hands along his stomach, revealing some sort of pocket built right into his skin.

"You're marsupials?" Brigid said.

"Excuse me?" Barbara glared at her.

Brigid quickly said, "It just means you have pouches that your young live in for a time while they're growing. Until they're ready to come out."

Barbara cocked her head to the side. "How do you know that?"

"There are many ani—" Brigid cut off whatever she'd been about to say, and instead said, "life forms on Earth who reproduce that way."

"Really?" Barbara smiled broadly at Craig. "How did we not know that? Earth is truly amazing in its biodiversity."

"Perhaps we can discuss this later," Craig said, struggling to hold on to the nestling's appendage.

As curious as Dane was about Lyrian reproduction, every instinct he possessed told him to get the hell out of there. He grabbed Brigid's hand and pulled her to the door, hugging the wall to stay as far from the Lyrians as possible.

"Holler if you need us," he said.

"There will be hollering." Barbara grinned at them, but it just made him more eager to leave.

Craig laughed. "And you should absolutely *not* come when you hear it."

Brigid sped up so that she was in front of Dane, tugging him out the door.

Chapter Nine

Brigid paced back and forth in her bedroom, trying to figure out which of her new housemates were aliens. Aliens!

She suspected Vay was Sadirian, just from her odd mannerisms. From what Barbara had said about Earthlings and Sadirians "pair-bonding", that meant that Henry was the Earthling in that couple.

With Brendan and Kira, it wasn't as easy to say. Kira was in training, and Brendan was making all this super-advanced technology. Brigid figured he was probably the alien there.

And, of course, with her and Dane, she knew who the Earthling was.

Not that they were a couple.

She couldn't date an alien. Could she?

Vay was one of the sweetest people Brigid had ever met. Everyone she'd met at the lodge was nice. Even Barbara, the space-Sasquatch. The only person associated with Brendan that hadn't been extremely welcoming and kind was Zemanni.

Brigid froze, remembering how the scar around his neck had seemed to glow—and how she'd thought at the time that no one could survive such an injury. No one human.

Oh my God. He's an alien, too.

Was he the same as Dane? Could Dane survive injuries like that?

Brigid suppressed a shudder. She hoped she would never find out.

As if all this wasn't enough to process, there was a warship on the way. From the sound of things, the aliens on board the *Reckoning* were decidedly unfriendly.

"What have I gotten myself into?" she whispered.

At least all the strange howling had stopped. She hoped that Craig and Barbara—and their nestling—were okay.

"This situation is so weird."

Someone knocked on the door, and she jumped. After taking a moment to calm herself, she called out, "Who's there?"

"It's me."

Dane's voice. She would recognize the low timbre anywhere now, even after such a short time. Her heart skipped and her skin tingled from the sound. Her brain might be conflicted, but her body seemed to be all-in where he was concerned.

I can't date an alien.

She took a deep breath, then let it out slowly. "Come

in."

Dane stepped into her room. He closed the door behind him. For a few moments, they just stood there, staring at each other.

"Were you ever going to tell me?" she said.

His voice was even lower than usual when he replied. "I was hoping I'd never have to. Brendan said at dinner you're only here for a couple of weeks. If I could've just kept my hands to myself, it wouldn't have been an issue."

"You were going to walk away from…"

She stopped, shaking her head. What exactly would he be walking away from?

They had amazing chemistry, and everything she'd learned about him so far she loved—*admired*. She admired.

Crazy timelines for other couples aside, there was no way she was ready to be throwing around the "L" word, even in her thoughts. She couldn't believe how much it stung that he seemed so willing to drop everything that had passed between them, though.

"A lot of the others are making this work," he said. "But I know better than to try. I shouldn't have let any of that stuff happen earlier, and I'm sorry for that."

"I'm not." The words slipped out. She couldn't bring herself to try to take them back.

His lips parted slightly and he leaned away from the door. But then his expression hardened and he looked down.

Some perverse part of her brain wouldn't let this go. "If the others are making it work, why do you think we can't?"

"They only think they're making it work," he said. "They don't know what the Coalition is willing to do to keep control. The lengths the High Council will go to. It's better not to risk it."

"There's always risk involved in living."

Point in case, her tossing the job she'd been trying for in Australia and taking this one instead. But she wouldn't have met Dane or the others if she hadn't taken Brendan up on his offer. She wouldn't know that aliens were real. As scary as it was, she realized it was also exhilarating.

"I'm glad I know," she said. "About you and Vay and Brendan and the others. I... I want to help." She made the decision as the words left her lips, resonating in her chest and making the skin on her face prickle.

It was absolutely terrifying to put herself out there like that. She didn't even know what she could do for them. She just knew she wanted to be part of this. Something meaningful, at last.

If there was an invasion force coming or aliens walking among Earthlings, she wanted to know what to do to keep her planet safe. Her family, her friends.

"Before you commit yourself to this, you need to know what we're dealing with." The color leached from Dane's face. "What the others don't even know."

"I'm listening," she said, trying to keep her voice calm

and level.

"You can't tell anyone. Not anyone here. Not anyone you know."

"I won't."

"Swear it." He pushed off from the door and stalked over to her, towering so close she could feel the heat from his body. "Swear it on whatever you hold most sacred."

She didn't hesitate to respond. "I swear on my family. My sister. I won't tell anyone. There's nothing more important to me."

"Good. Then I know I can trust you with this." He reached out and took her hands in his. "You'll understand what's really at stake."

A knot formed in her stomach. She just nodded, waiting for him to explain.

"From what I've been able to find, my parents were miners in an asteroid field near Alpha Lyncis," he said. "They lived in the dome the Coalition had built there. It was a small operation—just the two of them. They never logged a pair-bond, but kept volunteering to remain, even when their assignments were up."

He paused and cleared his throat before going on. "There was an accident at the site. When the Coalition arrived to help, the first thing they did was put them both in regen beds to scan them and heal their injuries." He let out a mirthless laugh. "I can't imagine how surprised the med-techs were to find that my mother was pregnant."

Brigid smiled, though something was nagging at the back of her mind. "Barbara said that Sadirians are genetically engineered."

Dane half-shrugged. "Sadirians might use maturation chambers, but physiologically, we're almost identical to Earthlings. The Coalition does everything it can to control *everything*. The food we eat, the air we breathe. Right down to our DNA."

"What did they do?" she asked, though she was dreading the answer.

"Coalition technology can do amazing things," he said. "My parents received mind-wipes so they wouldn't remember anything about their assignment together. And the med-techs transferred us to maturation chambers to finish our development."

The blood rushed from Brigid's head. Of all the things she imagined, that had not been one of them.

"Wait... 'us'?" she said.

Dane let out another of those sad laughs. "Yeah, that was the other surprise. I have a brother. A twin."

"What?" Brigid gasped.

"Guess we have more in common than you thought." His lip twitched up on one side. "Somehow, my brother and I were on the same space station at the same time. The genetic engineers don't make clones. The High Council wants to preserve our biodiversity. When Marq and I saw each other, we knew there was a connection. It's taken us years to figure this all out."

"That's amazing…and terrible," she said. "Do you ever get to see each other or talk?"

"We've done our best to hide how similar we look so we can meet every once in a while."

"You must have been so happy when you met," she said, trying to find some way to comfort him.

"I was. But Marq is part of a group of elite fighters selected by the High Council to have his emotions suppressed."

"That's…also awful," she said.

"Seeing me broke through Marq's conditioning." Dane's expression finally brightened a bit. "It started us on the path to restoring his emotions and figuring out what other things the High Council has been doing—and they've done a hell of a lot worse than what they did to us."

"Does anyone else know about this?" she said.

He let go of her hands, but only to grip her arms instead. "No one does—except Marq and now you."

"I can't believe you're trusting me with this."

"I have to. Because if you're going to stay and help us, I won't be able to stay away from you. I'm not strong enough. And you have to know what you're risking. What they're capable of. Wiping your memories is the least of what they could do to you. You can still walk away."

"No, I can't," she said. "This is my planet. I want to protect it."

Even if she didn't want to stay involved to protect her family, hearing his story would have convinced her to help. No one should have had to go through that. The Coalition needed to be stopped.

And Dane... Dane needed her. She could see it in his eyes, as much as she felt the answering need within her heart. Whether it was the weird pair-bonding between Earthlings and Sadirians or fate or whatever, she'd never been more certain of anything.

They belonged together.

He let out a little laugh and shook his head. "Beautiful and brave. I don't know that I deserve you."

"Life is full of risks," she said. "And this—you—are worth it."

Chapter Ten

Dane was stunned for a moment. He had always been treated as a tool—like all his fellow soldiers. No one had ever really wanted him before.

Until Brigid.

She reached up and gripped his face, pulling him down for a kiss that shook him to his soul. The passion they'd shared earlier was nothing compared to this. They devoured each other, tongues dancing, breath mingling.

He lifted her up and she wrapped her legs around his waist tight. Staggering forward a few paces, he reached the bed and fell onto it, careful not to crush her with his weight.

Having her beneath him felt too good. Too right.

He thrust against her as she groaned, squeezing her legs around him even tighter, holding him closer. They slid up the bed together, lips still exploring, limbs tangling. When they reached the pillows, he reared back, but only long enough to pull his sweater and the undershirt he wore beneath it over his head and toss them away.

Brigid hissed in a breath, her hands suddenly on his

chest and abdomen. His skin rose in goosebumps as she raked him with her nails.

He pinned her down again, letting more of his weight press her into the mattress, claiming her mouth once more. Her hands didn't stop moving.

She trailed her fingertips up his back, mixing light scratches with soothing touch. He'd never felt anything like the arcs of electric pleasure that raced along his nerve endings from what she was doing.

She released the lock her legs held on his waist, wrapping them around his thighs instead. Her hands slid down beneath his waistband, clutching his ass as he thrust against her.

His dick was throbbing almost painfully. He was afraid he'd climax any moment. He wanted this to last.

He shifted his weight onto his elbow, reaching for one of her arms to pull it away and try to slow things down, but she used the opportunity to push on his chest and roll him onto his back. He went along with it, letting out a low moan as she straddled him and sat up, pressing her core against his dick.

Closing his eyes, he fought to get his body at least a little bit under control. Then he heard the soft rasp of her clothes against her skin, and the thump of whatever she'd removed hitting the floor.

He almost didn't want to look. It would make resisting that much harder. Instead, he ran his shaking hands over her hips, sliding them up to her waist. All he met was smooth, warm skin.

He had to see. Opening his eyes, he found her staring at him, lips swollen, eyes wide, as if she was as awestruck by this connection as he was. That look kept him grounded, helped him back away from the edge they were both hurtling toward.

He reached up to cup her cheek, sitting up and bringing their chests together. The soft fabric of her bra rubbed against his chest as he kissed her slowly, deeply.

She shifted away from him a bit so she could angle her arms behind her and unclasp the undergarment. He felt her wriggle out of it and toss it away as well, then she pressed her chest against his again.

This was so much better. Nothing between them, the warmth of their skin mingling. He wanted more.

Wrapping his arms around her back, he rolled them over so he was on top of her again. He reached between them to undo her jeans, then started to tug them down over her full hips.

She'd already taken off her shoes, so it was easy to slide down along her body, pulling her clothing with him. He cast her jeans onto the floor, then quickly pulled off her socks.

Brigid lifted herself on her elbows, watching him. He kissed her legs as he made his way back up the bed, nuzzling the tender skin on the inside of her thighs. When he reached her panties, he hooked his fingers in their waistband, slowly pulling them down her legs.

His breath hitched as her soft curls were exposed, the scent of her arousal hitting him like a blow to the chest. He couldn't wait to bury himself in her, to feel her clench around him. But he had to regain more control.

This wasn't like using *Coupling*—the Coalition drug designed to control their citizens' sexual needs. This was just him and Brigid. This was real.

If he threw himself back on top of her, the rough fabric of his jeans could hurt her. He wanted to feel her skin against his. He wanted to feel her heat.

He slid to the foot of the bed, pulling her panties past her ankles and feet, then dropping them. He unlaced his boots in record time, then kicked them off and pulled off his own socks before standing again.

Taking a deep breath to return more self-control, he slowly undid the fastener of his jeans.

"Wait," Brigid said.

He froze. Was she having second thoughts?

His heart stuttered at the thought, his dick giving a painful pulse of disappointment. He might need a dose of *Coupling* after all if she changed her mind—just in the privacy of his own room.

"Come over here," she said.

Hopeful, he walked around the bed to where she gestured. She swung her legs over the side, then slid to her knees. She reached for his jeans, slowly pulling them down to his ankles so he could step out of them.

His erection pressed against the fabric of his boxer-briefs, held to his stomach by the uncomfortable elastic of the waistband. He completely forgot the mild discomfort as she ran her fingers along his shaft.

Pleasure like a shock cannon went off deep in his belly. His dick pulsed, sending more of those arcs of electricity through his body.

"I'm on birth control," Brigid said. "Just so you know."

"Okay." His brain only half-registered what she was talking about, the heat she was building within him consuming his thoughts.

"And I've been tested recently," she went on. "I know you don't like the regen beds, but are you safe to... You know. Do this?"

"Safe?"

Mentioning the regen beds had grounded him a little, pulling him back again from that glorious edge. He shook his head, trying to figure out what she was talking about. What would make sex unsafe on a planet at Earth's med-tech level?

"Are you talking about pathogens?" he said.

She half-smiled up at him. "That's a nice word for it. Yes, that's what I mean."

"We were all treated and cleared of anything that might be harmful to Earthlings or anything on Earth that might harm us if we're exposed to it."

Her smile grew. "I was so hoping you'd say that."

She gripped the waistband of his boxer-briefs and pulled them down to the floor. As soon as they were off, she gripped his dick firmly and slid her tongue along its length.

"Fuck," he gasped.

"That's the idea." She grinned up at him, then wrapped her lips around his crown, drawing him deep into her mouth.

The pleasure he'd experienced up to that point was nothing next to this. The currents of stimulation turned into a sustained blast cantering along his nerves, overloading his senses.

Was this how Earthlings had sex? He'd thought it was more like how Sadirians coupled.

No, that didn't make sense. Their anatomy was too similar for this to be—

His thoughts cut out as she slid him from her mouth almost completely, then drew him back in. Pressure built within him, a release so close he could almost touch it.

On one of her strokes, she released him, then shifted herself back onto the bed. He stood a moment, almost paralyzed, pleasure still beating against his mind, the longing to complete what they'd started almost unbearable.

She reached out to him and he took her hand, letting her pull him onto the bed.

Thank the stars.

That must have been a prelude—how Earthlings prepared their bodies for sex. What would he need to do for her?

He'd used *Coupling* with and without partners many times, but the drug took care of everything for them. Tactile stimulation was unnecessary, though he only used it with people who enjoyed full contact during its use.

This was so far beyond that.

What Brigid had done with her mouth simulated sex. It was galaxies away from relying on biochemical controls.

She buried her fingers in his hair, kissing him again, her tongue sliding along his lips. He met her invitation, delving deep within her mouth. Another simulation.

He held his weight up on one arm while he ran his free hand over the gentle curve of her stomach. She was so much softer than his previous partners had been. And without using *Coupling*, he had time to enjoy her, to explore her. Time he could use to help prepare her body for them to join.

He lifted one of her breasts, feeling the weight of it in his hand and squeezing its softness. Her quick intake of breath encouraged him. She had brought him so much pleasure with her touch.

He skimmed the backs of his fingers over her stomach as he made his way to her core. Wetness and heat greeted him. His dick throbbed as he imagined what it would feel like to slide into that part of her.

He needed to simulate the experience, as she'd done for him—to test her body for readiness and make sure she enjoyed this coupling every bit as much as he did.

Carefully, he slid one finger along her slit, gathering moisture. She moaned against his mouth, and he deepened his kiss, thrusting in with his tongue as he pushed his finger deep into her sex.

She clenched around his finger and arced up against his chest. He rolled slightly, putting more of his weight on her to keep her where he wanted her.

She was still too tight. He slid his finger free, then added another. Brigid grabbed his back, clawing at him as she tried to pull him closer.

He moved his hand against her, rubbing her clitoris with the heel of his palm as he thrust his fingers in and out. Her grip on his back tightened. His dick was throbbing, begging to take the place of his hand.

She let out a whimper, and he quickly pulled away, staring down at her to see if he'd hurt her.

"Please, Dane," she said. "I need you. Now."

She wrapped her leg around his thigh, pulling him farther on top of him. He didn't need more encouragement than that.

He settled against her core, barely parting her flesh, trying to catch his breath, to remember every flicker of pleasure on her face, every sensation they were sharing. Brigid slid her hands down to his ass, fingers digging in as she writhed beneath him, trying to draw him into her.

He couldn't wait any longer. In a fluid stroke, he drove himself into her, felt her body welcome him and hold him tight—as if she would never let him go.

He wanted to stay like that forever, but the need for more was too great to resist.

Pulling himself back till they were almost parted, he savored every pulse of energy their bodies shared. He could feel her body coiling beneath him, pressure building in his abdomen.

He crashed back into her, grabbing one of her thighs and holding it tight, using it to press himself as deep into her as he could. She let out a low, guttural, moan that called to something in him that he'd never encountered.

All thoughts left his mind. There was only heat and slickness and movement and *need* as he rocked against her.

His fingers dug into her leg even as her nails raked along his back. His thrusts became faster, almost frenzied as he slammed into her. The pressure in his abdomen increased until he thought he might explode. His body was just heat and pleasure and this union.

The room seemed to blank out just as she arched beneath him and cried out, her head writhing against the pillows. Her core clenched his dick as he kept pounding into her, pulsing in time with the shockwaves of pleasure that coursed through his body.

He felt himself spilling into her, his skin electrified, his muscles molten, his heart pounding in his ears. Finally, he stilled, buried deep within her, her arms and legs holding him as tightly as where they were joined.

He nuzzled her neck, breathing in her scent, and let himself be lost in her.

Chapter Eleven

Brigid woke up feeling more relaxed than she'd ever been. She was also sore in lots of…interesting places.

As tired as she'd thought she was the night before, she'd still had plenty of energy to introduce Dane to a wide variety of Earthly delights. She couldn't wait to do even more today—in the kitchen.

She looked at the clock and bolted upright as she saw the time. "Oh no."

"What?" Dane's speech was slurred as he hurriedly sat up next to her. "What is it?"

"We missed breakfast."

"Breakfast?" He shook his head. "Everybody has cereal for breakfast. It's one of the few things I cooked right, apparently."

"So, like, oatmeal?"

"No, like, out-of-the-box. The crunchy sweet stuff you pour milk over."

She tried not to laugh, but couldn't help it. "I'm so sorry. This is just… This is the weirdest job I've ever had. It still kind of feels like a dream."

"I'm with you there." He leaned over and kissed her.

It was light at first, but then he brought one of his hands to the back of her neck. The feel of his warmth, his strength, lured her in and she kissed him back. Deeper.

He was just starting to push her against the pillows when she remembered herself. She leaned away, smiling at him.

"I have a job to do," she said.

"So do I." At her questioning look, he went on. "My job is to make sure people are feeling good. And I think I can make you feel very good."

She laughed, but quickly slid out of the bed when he reached for her again. "I'm well aware of that fact. You can make me feel good *after* we have our own breakfast and make lunch."

Dane fell back against the pillows. "I never thought I'd appreciate nutrient bricks."

"What are nutrient bricks?" Brigid started going through her luggage, pulling out clothes and tugging them on.

"They're just what they sound like. Compressed nutrients that are easily created and consumed. Standard rations for citizens and soldiers alike."

Brigid scowled as she tried to imagine what that was like. "What kind of flavor do they have? Are they textured?"

"I'd say they're kind of like really dense sand."

"Ew. Wait, texture or taste?"

"Both."

She suppressed a shudder. After learning what the Coalition had done to Dane and his family, forcing all of the people in their civilization to eat dirt was completely believable.

"Don't take this the wrong way," she said, "but I really kind of want to kick the Coalition's butt."

Dane arced an eyebrow at her, then let out a huge laugh. "You and me both."

"You need to train me on how to fight. And to shoot a ray gun." She paused with one leg in her jeans. "I'm assuming you use ray guns."

All the mirth had left his expression when she glanced over at him. He slid from the bed and started to pull his own clothes on.

She finished getting into her jeans, then hurried over to him. "Did I say something wrong? Do you not use ray guns?"

"Yeah, we have ray guns, but I don't want you anywhere near them. When the *Reckoning* arrives, you need to be long gone from here."

"Are you kidding?" She let out a flat laugh. "We're in this together. I thought you understood that when we talked last night."

"The Coalition will erase your memory of me if they catch you—or worse."

She crossed her arms and glared at him. "Then don't let

them catch me."

He sighed. "I need you safe."

"I need you with me. Didn't you hear what Barbara said earlier about flash-fire pair-bonds?"

"Brigid, pair-bonds mean we're married."

"Oh." She felt her cheeks heat. "Well, that's a little fast, but then what isn't with you and me. This—what we're feeling—it's special. It's once-in-a-lifetime. And even without that, we're talking about my planet. I have a right to fight for it. I have a right to fight for *us*."

"Are you sure you're a chef? Because that was a mighty fine speech."

She smiled, sensing his resolve weakening. "I'll make you a deal. I teach you how to cook, you teach me how to fight."

"You shouldn't need to know how to fight. The closest dropgate generator is in the Centaurus system." He paused, then said, "Dropgates are how we travel over vast interstellar distances. From what we know, the *Reckoning* hasn't even arrived through the gate in Centaurus yet. Once it does, it'll take them three more weeks to reach Earth. Besides, when they arrive, they should only head for our Florida base."

"How do you know that?"

"The lodge doesn't have any Coalition tech they can track and target."

"I still don't see the harm in teaching me how to fight,"

she said. "Just in case."

Dane didn't look convinced.

"Think about it," she said.

He nodded. "I'll think about it. Right now, though, all I can think about is food. You really wore me out last night."

She grinned, then wrapped her arms around his neck and pulled him down for a kiss. She trailed her lips to his ear, nibbling on his earlobe until she could feel the hard length of his erection pressed against her.

"Just wait till tonight," she whispered.

"That's a long way off."

"I'm sure we can keep ourselves busy." She trotted back to her bag, pulling out a ponytail holder and putting up her hair. When she looked over at Dane, he had his hands on his hips and was staring at the ceiling.

"I need a minute," he said.

"Oh, right. Sorry."

"Sure you are." He smirked at her. "You go on ahead. I'll catch up after checking on Barbara." His brow furrowed. "I guess I mean Craig, since he's the one carrying the nestling now."

"It's kind of like seahorses," she said.

"What now?"

"Seahorses."

He looked at her blankly.

"I keep forgetting you're not from Earth." She shook her head. "My sister read every book about animals she could get her hands on when we were growing up. I used to read them with her. Seahorses are these adorable little animals that live in the ocean. The female puts her eggs in the male's pouch, and he fertilizes them and then gives birth to their babies when they're ready."

Dane shook his head. "I wish I had such extensive knowledge."

"I can ask Caitlin to recommend some books for you about marsupials. Or seahorses."

He smiled. "That's kind of you. I really don't know if any of them would help. Henry says his research tells him the closest life form on Earth to a Lyrian is something called a tardigrade."

"A water bear?"

He shook his head. "No, a tardigrade."

She laughed. "That's just another name for tardigrades. They're one of Caitlin's favorite animals, along with cuttlefish and donkeys."

Dane was staring at her blankly again. How could he possibly know what to make of all that? He probably didn't even know what cuttlefish or donkeys were.

Brigid settled on saying, "My sister is kind of weird."

She dredged up everything she knew about tardigrades both from her sister's books and the sci-fi stories that drew on them. Aside from her sister finding them adorable—which Brigid did not understand—Caitlin was most impressed with how incredibly tough they were.

Tardigrades were almost impossible to kill.

Brigid made a mental note to stay on Craig and Barbara's good side.

"I better get to the kitchen." She started toward him to give him a kiss, but he held up a hand to warn her off.

"Unless you're planning on going back to bed for a while, you better leave me be," he said.

She grinned, then hurried out the door. If she was going to make a lunch worthy of impressing her new boss, she didn't have any time to waste.

Her heart was pounding, and even with everything she'd learned, she couldn't remember the last time she'd been so happy. She wasn't sure she ever had been.

Okay, sure, there was the looming threat of an alien invasion—and the fact that Earth had apparently already been colonized by an alien race of lizard people. But she still felt more hopeful about her future than ever. She was part of something bigger than herself.

She wished she had time to make Dane a special breakfast, especially after wearing him out the night before. But cereal would have to do.

Her cheeks hurt from her smile as she opened the cabinets in the kitchen that held the bowls. She pulled out two of them, then turned and set them on the counter.

Unsurprisingly, there were a variety of cereals available to choose from, most of the boxes partially empty. From the sound of things, her fellow Earthlings had probably been eating a lot of it.

She shuddered at the thought of subsisting on nutrient bricks. No wonder Dane's cooking was so...odd. Everything must taste spectacular after only experiencing those. And he had no concept of which flavors should be alongside each other in a dish.

The night before had been utterly amazing. Dane had been eager to try out new things and learn everything he could. She wondered how that would translate in the kitchen.

For now, simple cereal, though. She opened a box, then rolled out the plastic bag inside as she turned toward the bowls.

A piercing noise startled her so badly that cereal flew out of the top of the box, hitting her in the face. She wheeled around, searching the room for the source of the sound, but it seemed to come from everywhere.

It wasn't like Barbara's screech, though that joined the horrible cacophony after only a few seconds. This was mechanical. It sounded like an alarm.

Brigid dropped the box of cereal and ran to the windows that lined the kitchen wall. A group of large shadows flitted over the trees—one circular and two rectangular. They were too regular in shape to be natural.

She couldn't see what was causing them, but whatever it was had to be big. Bigger than Zemanni's helicopter, that was for sure. She could only think of one thing.

"Ships…"

Spaceships.

A bright flash of light nearly blinded her, just before she heard a high-pitched whining sound. Her stomach felt like it had turned to ice.

The house shook as a thunderous crash sounded from somewhere below. She heard more booms and high-pitched whines, along with Barbara screeching.

"Oh no." She had to get to the others—to get to Dane.

Wheeling around, she ran to the rack that held several pots, pans, and skillets. She grabbed one of the skillets, then pulled a large butcher knife from the block of knives on the counter. She was nearly to the kitchen door when someone almost barreled into her.

She screamed and lashed out, recognizing Dane a moment too late. He leapt out of range of the knife, eyes wide.

"Whoa there," he said. "It's just me."

"Oh my God. I'm so sorry." She dropped the knife, but held onto the skillet, even when he pulled her into a crushing hug.

"I'm the one that's sorry." He kept holding her for way too long.

"Dane, we have to move," she said. "We have to get to the others."

She felt him shake his head as he held on. Her thoughts were spinning as she tried to think of ways she could help.

"It's too late for that," Dane said. "There's nowhere we could run to in time. Nothing we can do. They're going to take us, and if we try to fight back, they'll kill us." He buried his face in the nape of her neck. "I'm so sorry."

Brigid managed to get her hands between them and shoved him away. "Stop feeling sorry for yourself and start thinking," she shouted. "I'm not ready to give up."

"That's because you don't know what you're up against."

"Neither do they."

"They have weapons. Ships. Trained soldiers who will just as soon disintegrate us as look at us. They've probably had their emotions suppressed, so they won't even feel a damn bit of remorse."

"You told me last night only the elite fighters have their emotions suppressed," she said.

"What does that have to do with anything?"

"Would they send elite fighters to the lodge when all that..." she waved her hand at him, "fancy technology you mentioned last night is in Florida?"

"I... No, they wouldn't."

"I can work with that." She ran to the fridge and threw it open. "There has to be something in here we can use."

"Brigid, that's just food. There's nothing that can help us avoid being captured."

"Okay, then we need to sneak stuff on board with us that will help." She glared at him over her shoulder. "Think,

Dane. There has to be a way we can use their ignorance against them. You put baked beans on spaghetti. Vay freaked out over red pepper flakes. I was planning to blow your minds with a baking soda volcano."

Wait... That was it. Maybe.

She scrambled around the kitchen, grabbing the ingredients she'd need and a few containers.

"They're not going to let you take that on board," he said.

"Why? It's just inert cooking stuff." Until it was mixed together in the right proportions.

"They'll be here any second."

"Then spend your time thinking up a story about why we need this," she said. "Like Earthlings have to have a special diet and I need my gear to feed us or we'll die or something." From what she'd learned of the Coalition, she wasn't sure that would be motivating enough. "Tell them we'll have sloppy emotions or barf on them or something."

His lips almost twitched into a smirk as he stared at her, clutching her full backpack to her stomach. A mischievous glint entered his eyes, and he outright smiled.

"I think I have an idea."

Chapter Twelve

The crashing and sounds of plasma fire from below had quieted. That only made Dane more nervous.

He'd been on his way to the basement when he saw the interceptors hovering outside through the first floor windows. They'd disintegrated a large patch of forest to land.

There was no way they would be able to conceal the landing site they created. If Commander Teisha was willing to leave that much evidence behind, Dane wondered if she even cared about being discovered—which meant they weren't just here to arrest, reassign, or mind-wipe everyone. They were here to bring Earth into the Coalition, ready or not.

His only thought had been to get to Brigid. They would take her memories of him, but maybe they'd leave his intact. He'd been hoping for a few more moments to hold onto, but now, thanks to her, he had a plan that might give them more time together. A small part of him even wondered if it might give them enough time for someone to come to their aid.

Marq was on the *Reckoning*. They had to be careful not to reveal their connection, but he might be able to help. And the Vegans just needed enough time to mobilize. Once Commander Teisha knew who she was dealing with, surely she'd change her plans.

Dane started to feel a glimmer of hope as he loosened the straps on Brigid's backpack for her, letting it hang lower on her body. He pulled off his sweater and handed it to her.

"Here, put this on," he said.

She glared at him. "Are you kidding me? This is your great plan?"

"Trust me. It's going to work."

He hoped so, anyway.

She sighed, but then struggled into his sweater, pulling it down over the backpack that she was wearing on the front of her body. He adjusted the sleeves a little, then pulled the lower hem down so the backpack was completely obscured —except for the large bulge right at her belly.

"This is ridiculous," she said.

"It isn't." He actually smiled. "No Sadirian has ever seen a pregnant female. They have no idea what one looks like."

"Are they all stupid and blind, too? Because it's pretty obvious this isn't actually my stomach. The outer pocket's zipper is making a line right here." She drew her finger across her stomach.

"They won't notice." When she just kept glaring, he added, "Marq and I have been in the same room together. No one realized we're twins and all I had to do was grow out my hair and darken it, leave some stubble, and get a tan."

"You're kidding."

"I'm not."

Her lips quirked up at one side. Maybe the hope he was feeling was contagious. They had to hold on to it.

But just in case, he leaned in and gave her a quick kiss. The temptation to deepen it welled up in him, but he heard the sound of footsteps in the hall and quickly turned to stand in front of her.

The first soldier ran into the room, disintegration pistol aimed at them. Dane held up his empty hands.

"We're unarmed," he yelled.

"What's that behind you?" the soldier said, a second joining him.

"Just an Earthling." Dane slowly stepped aside, revealing Brigid in all her "pregnant" glory.

Dane's burgundy sweater hung in loose wrinkles on her tiny frame, pulled tight across her backpack-belly. She held up her hands like Dane, eyes wide and skin even paler than usual. She must be terrified at the sight of the soldiers.

They wore the standard form-fitting silver uniform with opaque metallic helmet of all soldiers. Aside from easily determining that they were both male, all she could see in them was her own reflection, distorted from the curve of their faceplates.

He hated that she was going through this. How the hell had the *Reckoning* managed to get to Earth so quickly? The Department of Homeworld Security had solid data that the warship hadn't used the Centauri dropgate generator, and it was the closest one to Earth.

More misgiving fired in Dane's belly. Though the Centauri always seemed docile and obedient, following the High Council's orders, they were known to be on Earth. The Department of Homeworld Security had thought they were trespassing against Coalition law, but Dane was starting to wonder if maybe the High Council was more aware of their presence than they wanted to let on.

His more immediate concern was the two soldiers in the room with them. They both stiffened, their weapons poised and ready to fire.

"We're not resisting," Dane said. "And we're unarmed."

"What's wrong with her," the first soldier said. "She's all…bloated."

"Hey," Brigid yelled.

Dane slowly lowered his hands to her shoulders. "She's pregnant."

"Pregnant?" Both of the men in the silver jumpsuits recoiled.

"There's another Earthling growing inside of that one?"

the taller one said.

"Yes. And if you cause her too much distress, she might go into labor," Dane said.

"What does that mean?" The first soldier's hands were shaking.

This was definitely not an elite squad. That could work either for or against them.

These soldiers would be easier to manipulate. But if Dane pushed too far, he could set them off and make them act recklessly. He needed to proceed cautiously. Unfortunately, Brigid had other plans.

"Please." She rolled her eyes. "Labor is what we call it when a human woman is about to give birth to a child."

Even through their uniforms, Dane could hear the soldiers suck in a breath. They turned to face each other briefly, then looked back to Brigid. Their weapons lowered a bit.

"Oh, come on," Brigid said.

"Do you know what happens when an Earthling gives birth?" Dane took a careful step closer to the soldiers. "There's an organ in her body housing the infant—and it will explode."

The shorter soldier who had entered the room first actually took a step to the side, shifting himself behind the taller one.

Dane had them right where he wanted them.

"That is not true," Brigid said.

Dammit, she was going to ruin this. He turned to her, and said, "Really? What's the first thing that happens in labor? Your water breaks. And it splashes all over the place."

"No, it doesn't," Brigid said. "I mean... Well, I guess it can."

Dane turned back toward the soldiers. "You see? But it isn't actually water. It's a slurry of biological waste products and amniotic fluid."

"What?" Brigid yelled.

Dane went on, going into as much detail as he could about the entire process—and thankful that he'd been curious enough to do some research into Earth's natural reproductive process. The soldiers shrunk closer together as he spoke, gasping occasionally. A loud crash sounded from somewhere else in the house, but the soldiers barely seemed to notice.

"You're making this up," the taller one said.

"I wish I were," Dane said.

"Tell us the truth." The taller one pointed his gun toward Brigid. "Your reproduction process can't be that disgusting."

"It's not disgusting," she said. "It's natural. It's *beautiful*."

She was interrupted when the shorter soldier made a gagging sound.

"Cygnus X," he mumbled. "She didn't deny it."

"It doesn't matter what comes out with the baby," Brigid said. "The important thing is that it's a new life and—"

"Let's just leave her here," the short one said.

The tall soldier shook his head. "Our orders are to take everyone to the ship for mind-wipes and reassignments."

Dane's heart seemed to stutter. Just a day ago, of all the possible consequences of them being taken by the *Reckoning*, he would have considered that just about the best. Now, the idea of Brigid forgetting him, of being separated from her, was like a knife to the chest.

Dane grabbed her arms and pulled her against his chest. He wanted to remember every moment, but he also had to keep up the charade.

"Don't upset her, you fools," he said.

"This is ridiculous," Brigid said.

The tall soldier lowered his gun. "Let's just get them to the ship. Once she's aboard, she's the medical staff's problem."

Dane shook his head. "She's my patient. I'm the only one who has studied Earth childbirth and delivery."

"Okay," the tall one said. "We keep you together. But you're still coming with us to the ship."

Dane wrapped one arm around Brigid's shoulders and cradled her "belly" with his other hand. "It's going to be okay," he said. "Trust me."

Stars, how he hoped that was true.

The shorter soldier stepped aside, letting the other lead

them from the room. Dane could feel the man's gaze on their backs, even through the opaque metal of his helmet.

A set of windows and the wall surrounding them had been completely blown into the central entryway to the house. Glass and wood splinters covered the tile floor. Dane kept close to Brigid as the soldiers urged them through the opening.

Only one interceptor sat in the new clearing they had made by blasting a crater into the once-serene forest around the lodge. They must have thought the lodge would be an easy target—which wasn't far from the truth.

The main firepower was down in Florida. No one had thought the Montana base would be a target. The only fighting power they had was Craig and Barbara, and there was no way Dane wanted them in the line of fire. Not with a nestling on the way.

A shadow flickered across his eyes. He looked up to see a shuttle already departing. At first, he thought maybe they'd be led to the interceptor, but as they descended into the crater, he could see another shuttle off to the side.

Plasma fire sounded from back in the house. Everyone turned to see lights strobing out from a huge hole in one of the retaining walls—a basement wall. Rubble was strewn around the ground outside the hole. Barbara let out a screech that seemed to stab right through Dane's eardrums.

"No," Dane said.

Brigid started back toward the house, but the soldier at

the back of the line stepped forward, his plasma rifle pointed at her. Dane grabbed her arm and held her back.

"There's nothing we can do for them," he whispered.

"We can't just leave," she said.

"Get into the shuttle." The soldier shoved his gun at them, the menace in his voice evident.

Dane pulled Brigid to the ramp, passing the tall soldier whose faceplate was pointed at the lodge. As soon as they were on board, Dane helped Brigid onto one of the bench seats and started strapping her in.

"Dane, we can't just leave them," she repeated.

"I hate this just as much as you do," he said. "But if we try anything, they'll disintegrate us."

He glanced out at the soldiers standing at the foot of the ramp. The shorter one was angled so that he could see both the house and the exit from the shuttle. The taller was fixated on the lodge.

From their body language, Dane could tell the soldiers were using their communication systems to talk without being overheard. He was almost glad not to hear. He already knew the outcome. They were heading for the *Reckoning*, and there was nothing they could do about it.

The plasma fire died down. Silence pressed in on him, heavy enough he could barely breathe. Minutes passed that felt like hours. Finally, he heard people approaching.

"Up the ramp," someone barked.

Henry stumbled into the ship, holding a large brown

satchel that was almost as big as his torso. When one of the half-dozen soldiers with him moved toward it, he jerked away.

"Don't touch her," he yelled.

Dane's heart sank. What the hell did that mean?

Dane stepped forward and Henry flinched away at first. He blinked a few times, as if he didn't recognize Dane.

"It's me," Dane said.

Henry's gaze flitted over the shuttle, resting briefly on Brigid. Dane helped Henry to sit.

"Where's Vay?" Henry said.

"Another shuttle just launched." Dane sat next to Henry and started to buckle him in as he had Brigid.

The soldiers filed onto the shuttle. Dane's heart grew heavier with each one. Had they all been captured that easily?

As one of the soldiers passed them, he said, "I wish all our prisoners were as helpful as this one."

"Yeah, well… I wish you would get blown out an airlock." Henry glared at the soldier. "Yeah. I said it."

"What happened in there?" Dane asked.

Henry looked down at the satchel he was carrying, then glanced over at the soldiers briefly. His brow furrowed.

Raising his voice as if he was making sure everyone would hear, he said, "These heartless fiends killed Barbara."

Brigid gasped, but Dane almost laughed. It was

reflexive. He'd seen the weapons these soldiers were carrying, and none of them packed the kind of power it would take to kill a Lyrian.

Henry clung to the pod more tightly, squeezing it against his chest. Still using that strange tone, he said, "This is all that's left of her, and I won't part with it."

Holy crap… Was that a Lyrian stasis pod?

Dane had heard of them, but he'd never seen one up close. He shifted closer to Henry, wrapping his shoulders in a hug that put Dane's mouth right next to Henry's ear.

"Tardigrades," Dane whispered.

Henry nodded, and Dane caught the hint of an almost-smile.

"Tardigrades." Henry said.

Damn, this Earthling was smart. Henry cleared his throat, then forced his face into a scowl that would have been obviously fake to anyone who knew him.

Let the soldiers think they'd killed a Lyrian. It wouldn't be long before Barbara was shoving their bragging words down their mouths with one of her many hands.

"What about Craig?" Dane whispered.

Henry's voice was barely audible when he responded. "Escaped."

Thank the stars.

The fact that they were leaving meant the soldiers must not know about Craig at all. With the Lyrian's natural cloaking abilities, he and the nestling were undetectable. If

Craig could manage to contact the Florida base, so much the better.

But Craig couldn't use any of the technology on his ship. That would be a beacon for the *Reckoning*. Dane could only hope that Craig would figure out some other way to call for help.

Dane leaned back and squeezed Henry's shoulder. "I'm so sorry for your loss."

Henry just nodded, hugging Barbara's stasis pod closer as he plastered on a look of fake outrage. Well, mostly fake. He had to be freaking out inside that Vay wasn't with them.

"We're launching," one of the soldiers said. "Strap in."

Dane glanced over to see that everyone else on the ship was already seated on the benches along both sides of the shuttle, belted securely to the hull. Two of the soldiers were up front, prepping to depart.

Most of the soldiers must have stayed behind to help with Barbara. Even so, Dane doubted Vay would be able to take on the ones that were on her shuttle. He just hoped that Brendan was with her.

"This is so terrible." Brigid was staring at Henry, her eyes filled with unshed tears.

Dane sat in one of the empty spaces next to her, leaving the last seat on the side closest to the hatch vacant. The soldiers who captured them had probably already warned the others about the "pregnant" Earthling and they were keeping their distance.

Dane quickly secured his harness, then reached for Brigid's hand and interlaced their fingers. Reassuring her would be harder without tipping off the others, but he had to try. He waited for the shuttle to launch, letting the inertia of the takeoff shift him closer to her.

"How much do you know about tardigrades?" he asked. She glanced over at him and he gave her the biggest smile he could manage.

She glared at him, her mouth falling open. "What does that have to do with—"

"Brigid," he said. "Think about it."

She looked over at Henry, who glanced down at Barbara's stasis pod, then flashed her a quick grin. Her eyes widened. The soldiers might not be able to see Dane's expression, but they could see hers.

"Don't let yourself get too upset." He purposefully spoke up, wanting everyone to hear. "We wouldn't want you to go into labor."

He looked back at the soldiers to see them shrinking away in their seats, trying to get as far from her as possible. Only a couple were looking at her, and even without seeing their faces, they were radiating tension and fear.

"I'm glad they kept us together." Dane locked his gaze with Henry's willing him to understand their ruse. "It'll be good to have an Earthling biologist to assist me with Brigid's care. Most Sadirians don't even know what a pregnant life form looks like."

Henry looked over at the soldiers, his lips tightening as if he was suppressing a laugh. He quickly contorted his features back into despair, then nodded.

"Yes, I will be happy to assist you." He spoke woodenly, but the soldiers didn't seem to pick up on it.

Now if only their luck would hold.

Chapter Thirteen

A door opened in the back of the shuttle, the hatch lowering toward the ground to act as a ramp. Through the opening, Brigid could see a dull metallic gray floor.

She felt like she might throw up. If she did, she wanted to hit as many of these jerks as possible.

The soldiers would be even more hasty getting out of the ship if they knew her thoughts. As it was, they all seemed to be scrambling to get away from her and out of the ship.

Dane unhooked his harness, then knelt in front of her as he started to unstrap her from the bench.

"You doing okay?" he asked.

"Do I look like I'm doing okay?" she snapped.

He smirked, a deep dimple appearing in the side of his face. She wanted to trace it with her fingertips, to feel the reassuring rasp of his stubble against her skin. Instead, she sat there, feeling disconnected, knowing she was probably in some kind of psychological shock.

At least Barbara wasn't really dead. Or Brigid *thought* so anyway. She couldn't imagine Henry and Dane looking so calm otherwise.

Dane turned to help Henry with his harness. When Henry smiled at him, Dane shook his head and made a point of grimacing.

"Oh, right," Henry said.

His face returned to the almost comical mask of sadness as he held…whatever that was in his arms. Brigid was glad the soldiers were either rock-stupid or not paying enough attention to notice the exchange.

"Come on." Dane gripped her arm and urged her to stand.

"Where are they taking us?" Brigid asked.

"The brig, probably," he said.

Henry's face brightened. "Will Vay be there?"

"I don't know." Dane shook his head. "But we need to follow instructions or risk being vaporized. All of us here are considered expendable."

"Even you?" Brigid shifted closer to him.

"Especially me," he said. "Med-techs are easily replaced. They'll want to interrogate you both to find out if anyone else needs a mind-wipe, but don't think that makes you safe."

Her stomach cramped again, worry flooding her system. "Won't they want to interrogate you, too?"

Dane smirked. "Right now, they just want me to take care of you. As long as I do that, they probably will barely notice me at all. Which is just the way I like it." He added the last bit under his breath.

Henry stood and followed them as they exited the shuttle. He stopped next to her, both of them staring up at the hangar bay.

"This should be so cool," Henry said.

"Yeah." She totally understood where he was coming from.

The room was huge, with half a dozen shuttles and three of those big flying-saucer looking ships filling it. At the far end, she could see a large opening in the wall, and beyond that a field of black speckled with stars.

"Wow," she said. "We're really in space."

"Move," someone barked.

The approaching soldiers held what looked like high-tech rifles. It was so eerie seeing her face distorted in their helmets.

She glared at them. "You don't have to be so pushy."

"Let's do what the man with the plasma rifle says." Dane wrapped one arm around her waist and started heading across the hangar. "Come on, Henry."

"Coming." Henry's voice sounded almost upbeat. Staring out at the stars seemed to have lifted his spirits.

They were led through an archway and down a series of halls with plain white walls and a dull gray floor that matched the one in the hangar. The ship was depressingly nondescript—no decoration, no personality at all.

She shivered as she imagined what it must be like living

on it. Was this what Dane had dealt with his entire life?

They had to find a way out of this. She couldn't stand the thought of him returning to that existence.

"In here." The soldiers stopped before a large opening. Inside, there were benches along the walls and nothing else.

"Are you kidding me?" Brigid said. "There's not even a toilet in there. Or don't you have those in space?" She sneered at them, but the soldiers didn't seem to mind.

"Brigid, it's okay." Dane stepped closer, urging her inside.

"That's easy for you to say," she huffed. "You're not *pregnant*."

He smirked, that dimple reappearing. "There's a panel that leads to a bathroom. I can show you."

She cast one last withering glare at the soldiers as she stepped into the room with Dane. Henry followed.

A buzzing sound started up. When she looked back, the hallway beyond the arch was blurred. Some kind of flickering energy blocked the doorway.

"I'm guessing we shouldn't touch that," she said.

"Yeah, that wouldn't be a good idea." Dane crossed the room, then ran his hand over the wall. A door slid aside, revealing a small bathroom.

"I don't actually need to use the bathroom, I just wondered where it was," she said.

"We should probably give you a check-up, don't you think?" Dane angled his head toward the small room.

Maybe he had a plan. Or maybe he just wanted a moment alone with her.

"I'll need your help, Henry," Dane said.

So much for that idea.

"Oh, okay," Henry said.

They all crammed into the small room. Dane tapped something on the wall and the door shut.

"One thing you can count on with Sadirians," Dane said. "They do everything they can to try to ignore anything that deals with bodily functions."

"So, what, there's no surveillance in here?" Brigid glanced around the room, but all she saw was nondescript metal and white paneling. There wasn't even a mirror.

"There's also no way out, unless you plan to squeeze down a drain or shimmy through an air vent," Dane said. "And even if you make it out, the ship's sensors can find you and lock you down the moment someone realizes you're gone."

"If they can't hear us, can you please explain exactly what has happened to Barbara?" Brigid asked.

Dane smiled at her as he reached out to squeeze her shoulder. He shifted closer, his face tilting toward hers with a look that made her toes curl.

"Um, I'd like to know more about that, too." Henry's voice broke in. He wasn't smiling anymore. "She told me she'd be okay and to keep her with me no matter what. But they hit her with so much firepower…"

"Unless they managed to throw her into an engine core, I think she'll be fine." Dane took the pod and set it on the small counter. The chitinous exterior gleamed in the light, a dark brown with swirls of gold. "I've never seen a Lyrian in stasis before."

"I'd rather see her *out* of stasis," Henry said.

The pod began to rock.

Dane inched back, pulling Brigid with him. "Looks like you're about to get your wish."

"Could she be coming out of stasis already?" Henry asked.

"I don't know," Dane said. "But maybe let's give her some space."

Henry nodded, then pressed himself against the wall along with the others.

Cracks streaked across the pod's surface. They widened as the rocking became more vigorous.

Two white-furred hands appeared in one of the openings, prying it farther apart. Then two more. With a shrill yell, Barbara split open the pod, both halves flying off the counter and bouncing off the walls.

She stood in the sink, her chest heaving as she bared rows and rows of shark-like teeth at them and screamed, the small sound not nearly as scary as her earlier screeches. She blinked a few times, closing her mouth as she stared at them.

"Henry, when did you get so big?" she asked.

"Um, Barbara?" Brigid said. "You got small."

The once gigantic Lyrian was about the size of a chimpanzee. A small one, at that. Her fur was fluffier than it had been before and a more vibrant white. The blue skin on her face and ears had paled to a sky blue.

She looked adorable.

Brigid knew better than to say anything about that. Barbara's teeth might be smaller, but she still had tons of them, and they looked sharper than ever.

Barbara looked at her hands—all four of them—and gasped. "No, no, no. I stayed behind to protect Henry. How can I do anything like this?"

Henry grabbed her up in a hug and buried his face in the fur on the side of her head. Dane had told Brigid that Henry had only lost his human parents less than a year ago. Even though he knew Barbara was tough as a tardigrade, this still had to have been frightening.

"Don't worry about that," Henry said. "I'm just glad that you're okay."

"Barbara, can you cloak yourself when you're this size?" Dane asked.

"I can," she said.

He nodded. "When Lyrians are cloaked, you're undetectable, right? Even to Sadirian scanners?"

Barbara's lips stretched into a grin. "Completely."

"I do not like the sound of this," Henry said.

Brigid wasn't sure she did, either. But she liked the idea

of staying locked up even less.

"Oh, nestling, don't worry." Barbara clasped Henry's cheeks with two of her hands, holding onto his shoulders with the others. "I've done much worse in my time." She turned back to Dane. "I take it you have a plan?"

"I'm starting to," he said. "With the group we have, we just might be able to pull it off."

Chapter Fourteen

"That's not a plan," Brigid said, scowling. "That's what you do when a plan fails."

Henry and Barbara didn't look too pleased with Dane's idea, either. The Lyrian was sitting on Henry's shoulders, one set of arms holding on to Henry's head for balance and the other set crossed over her chest.

"You didn't like my backpack-pregnancy plan either, but look at us now," Dane said.

"Yeah, look at us." Brigid gestured to her backpack sitting in the sink. "We're all crammed into a bathroom. But everything will be okay, because we snuck the ingredients for a baking soda volcano on board."

"A baking soda volcano?" Henry asked. "Why?"

"I was pressed for time and kind of panicking," Brigid said.

Henry had a far-off look in his eyes. "No, that's actually a great idea. Vay is more easily distracted than most Sadirians, but from my time with them, I think most would absolutely freak out it they saw one. Do you have food coloring?"

"Of course," Brigid said.

Henry nodded. "And how many containers did you bring?"

"Four," she replied. "They're different sizes."

"Do you guys want to clue me in on *your* plan?" Dane was feeling a little left out. "What the hell even is a baking soda volcano?"

"When you add certain common kitchen chemicals together in the right amounts, they have a sort of fizzing reaction," Henry said. "It can actually be really big."

Barbara hopped down from Henry's shoulders and started rummaging through Brigid's backpack.

"I'm familiar with these chemicals." Barbara chuckled. "Oh, this is hilarious. The mixture will be harmless, especially with Sadirian uniforms protecting them, but if we add these coloration packets, it'll look just like the acidic spit from a Cygnian vorrat. Any Sadirian we hit with this will be absolutely terrified."

"Barbara crawls through the vent, cloaked, like you planned," Brigid said. "But instead of just opening a communications channel in the cell so you can get your secret friend to find us a hiding place, she can set up one of our baking soda volcanoes near the guard. While he's distracted, she can open our cell and we can overpower him."

"That's too dangerous," Dane said.

"And you think waiting things out isn't?" Barbara snorted. "If your General Serath—pardon me, 'Adam Smith'—was successful in convincing the High Council to recognize Earth's first contact committee, they wouldn't have sent the *Reckoning* or taken everyone into custody immediately."

Dane's stomach sank. Barbara was giving voice to his worst fears. He couldn't let himself think about that at the moment. They were still near Earth. They could still be rescued.

"I'm trying to keep us alive here," Dane snapped. And hopefully keep their memories intact.

Barbara closed up Brigid's backpack. "I can easily take out a Sadirian soldier on my own even at this size."

"But she won't have to." Brigid gestured to the door. "We'll all help. Only one soldier stayed behind and we didn't pass anybody on our way here. We can make sure nothing's changed, then work on escaping."

"Or we can find a place to hide until the Vegans mobilize and negotiate our release." Dane still wasn't sure how much the soldiers aboard the *Reckoning* would hesitate before vaporizing any of them. It seemed too big a risk.

"We have to rescue Vay and Brendan," Henry said.

Dane shook his head. "Vay and Brendan aren't in danger. They're probably just being questioned."

"Maybe they're not in physical danger, but what do you think will happen to them once the Coalition gets the information they want?" Henry asked. "While we're standing around arguing, they could be getting mind-wipes."

Damn, Henry had a point.

"If we go out there, they could vaporize us on sight," Dane said. "They already tried to kill Barbara, and they have a hell of a lot more firepower on this ship. Would Vay want you to risk that? Would Brendan?"

Henry's lips pulled in a tight line. Henry had to know Dane was right.

But if their places were switched, Dane knew it wouldn't make a difference. As long as he knew Brigid was safe, he'd do whatever it took to save her memories of him.

"Do you think whoever you're trying to reach on board can stop them from getting their memories erased?" Brigid asked.

"I don't know, but he can try," Dane said.

"Who are you even trying to contact to help us find this hiding place?" Henry hunched over as Barbara crawled back onto his shoulders, then reached up and started messing with the vent above them. It didn't take her long to peel the grate open, leaving it dangling from the ceiling.

"The first officer is a friend of mine." Dane was afraid to say more. Even that admission felt like like too much.

"That's great." Henry actually smiled. "Then get him to let us go."

"It's not that simple," Dane said.

"Why not?" Henry grunted, distracted for a moment as Barbara reached behind him, the set of hands on his face coming dangerously close to poking him in the eyes. "Surely he can sneak us out or something. Sabotage the mind-wipe procedure."

That was a possibility, but also a risk. A huge risk. If Dane and Marq were discovered working together, it might lead to someone figuring out their true connection.

At the same time, Henry and Kira were looking at losing their bondmates. Sure, there was a chance when the dust settled they could be reintroduced and fall in love again, but what were the odds of that happening?

Dane knew he was being selfish, wanting to keep his bonds with Brigid and Marq safe, along with all of their memories. But if Dane let the others lose their pair bonds because he was too afraid to even try to help, how did that make him any better than the High Council?

Brigid reached out and rested her hand on Dane's chest. "What's complicating this?"

"The first officer of the *Reckoning* is Marq," Dane said.

"Oh." Her eyes widened. "Oh!"

"Who is Marq?" Henry asked.

"Oh no." Brigid covered her face with her hands. "Oh wow, this *is* complicated."

"Who is Marq?" Henry's voice rose.

Barbara suddenly leapt up from Henry's shoulders. She hung from the edge of the vent for a moment, Brigid's backpack dangling from one of her hands.

"Hey," Brigid said. "That's my backpack."

Barbara chucked the backpack into the vent, then gracefully pulled herself after it. Her face appeared in the opening an instant later.

"I'm sure you all will sort this out," she said. "But in the meantime, I have another nestling who needs me."

"What?" Henry said. "I thought Craig escaped."

"Not your brother." Barbara chuffed out a breath. "Your bondmate. I'm not leaving her to the non-existent mercies of the solder is on the *Reckoning*." She looked at Dane and added, "I'll make sure you get to chat with your little friend on the ship."

"Barbara, wait…" Dane reached up, but she vanished, activating her cloaking ability. He heard a shuffling sound from the vent, then nothing.

"Crap," Henry said.

"What do we do now?" Brigid shifted closer.

"I don't know." Dane wanted to pace, but there was barely room to turn around with all three of them in the bathroom.

What the hell did Barbara think she was even going to do out there?

He remembered Brigid's words from the night before. *"Life is full of risks."*

This was worth it. He couldn't let the love that Kira and Brendan and Henry and Vay had found be taken away.

"Okay," Dane said. "Henry and I will go back out into the main cell. Without your backpack, Brigid will need to stay in here so they don't notice that something is wrong. As soon as we see that the communications channel is open, I'll contact Marq and tell him—"

The door slid open behind them. Dane's stomach seemed to drop to his feet. He wheeled around, arms spread to protect Brigid.

No one was there.

"Ahem."

Dane looked down to see Barbara standing in front of them, all four arms crossed and one eyebrow ridge raised. She shook her head and made a tutting sound.

"Ridiculous Sadirians," she muttered. "So full of themselves."

"How..." Dane began.

"Haven't you read my file?" Barbara stepped back and gestured toward the room. "I'm a notorious smuggler with a huge bounty on my head for doing much more complicated things than this. Not to mention having four arms makes for quick work with simple chemicals like those."

"Where's my backpack?" Brigid asked, filing out of the bathroom with the others.

"I left it on the soldier's head." Barbara smiled, showing all of her sharp teeth. "It was very heavy and made an effective weapon once he'd started trying to strip out of his uniform."

Dane hurried to the opening to the cell. The force shield was gone. The Sadirian guard was lying on the floor, his uniform half-off and, as Barbara had said, Brigid's backpack sitting on his head.

"You might have moved it." Dane picked up the bag and handed it to Brigid. "We don't want to hurt anyone."

"Speak for yourself," Barbara said.

Dane couldn't use the bracer built in to the soldier's uniform to check his vitals, so he visually inspected the man for injuries. He'd have a hell of a headache when he woke up, but he seemed okay otherwise. An orange, viscous fluid was still bubbling on the side of his uniform.

That's a baking soda volcano?

It really did look like vorrat spit.

Dane stripped the soldier down to his undergarments, then dragged him into the cell. Brigid was squatting down by her pack with Henry. They had started pulling things from the pack and mixing them together in the containers she'd brought along.

"Dane is right," Brigid said. "We aren't here to hurt anyone. Besides, if the Vegans are going to be negotiating our release, we don't want to give the Sadirians on this ship any reason to deny them."

"The Sadirians on this ship will do whatever they damn well please." Barbara leapt onto the control console outside of the cell, hanging on with one arm and her feet. Her free hands flew over the controls.

"What are you doing?" Dane asked.

"Memorizing as many of the ship's schematics as I can while I have the chance." She shrugged. "And opening that communications channel you wanted. I'm using my own encryption pathways, but you'll need to use whatever code you have—and I truly hope you have one that will make your contact undetectable."

"Of course we do." Dane joined her at the console. As soon as she was done, he keyed in the code that would let him send a message to Marq.

Brigid looked up at them and asked, "What message are you going to send?"

His original idea was to let Marq know they were on the ship and ask for a place that they could ride this out safely. If he could get Marq to stall the mind-wipe procedure, that would be even better.

"I'm telling him to stop the mind-wipes," Dane said. "Whatever it takes."

He keyed in the message, then held his breath as he waited for a response.

Two words flashed on the screen. He knew Brigid and Henry couldn't read the Sadirian text, and was grateful. But now, it was on him to tell them the news.

"What is it?" Henry asked. "Dane, what did Marq say?"

Dane shook his head. "We're too late. The chamber is already active."

Chapter Fifteen

"Henry, stop!"

Dane kept yelling after Henry, both men sprinting down the hallway. Brigid could barely keep up.

She hefted her backpack onto her shoulders again, trying to keep it in place while she also held onto the canisters that she and Henry had been working with when Dane told them the news. They still didn't know who was in the chamber, but from the way Henry was running, he seemed sure it was Vay.

Barbara was leading them, somehow staying ahead of everyone. She would vanish from sight occasionally, then reappear to let them know the way ahead was clear.

The floor beneath her lurched suddenly, nearly knocking Brigid from her feet. Everyone staggered. Even Barbara stopped, looking at the walls. Alarms began to blare, red and gold lights flashing along the corridor.

"What was that?" Brigid said.

"Decompression alarms." Dane's eyes were wide. "Something hit the ship and took out part of the hull."

"I thought this was the toughest ship the Coalition had," she said.

"It is, apart from the *Arbiter*," Dane said. "It must be the Vegans."

Brigid's heart started to pound.

"Do they know we're on board?" Henry asked.

"I don't know," Dane said.

"Is it possible they'll try to destroy the ship?" she asked.

He shook his head. "I don't know."

"This changes nothing," Barbara said. "We must still reach the nestling."

She turned and started charging down the hallway again. As she did, she let out a high-pitched, slightly-less-terrifying version of her signature screech. Henry ran after her, a grim set to his face.

"Well, the Sadirians know we're here now," Brigid said.

Dane took her hand in his and squeezed it. Together, they ran after the others.

"The mind-wipe chamber isn't far," Dane said. "They're usually pretty close to the brig. We're lucky that whatever is going on outside is distracting the soldiers, or they probably would have found us by now."

"Right. Lucky." She pushed as much sarcasm into the word as she could, given that they were running flat-out and she could barely breathe.

"I can still find you a place to hide," Dane said.

She shook her head. "No way."

"I never knew I could love and hate something about someone so much at the same time," he said.

"What's that supposed to mean?" she managed, through several breaths.

"You're stubborn and brave."

"Oh. Okay then."

From far off in the ship, she heard the sound of rending metal. The walls around them made a terrible groaning sound, as if they were experiencing sympathy pains.

"Dane?" she said.

"It's just ahead."

That was great, unless the ship imploded or exploded or decompressed or whatever as soon as they got there.

Henry and Barbara didn't slow as they ran into a large, open room. It was octagonal, with small chambers connected to it and a couple of sealed doors leading who knew where.

The alarms and flashing lights were going off here, too. Brigid was glad, because it was distracting the Sadirians scrambling around.

These soldiers didn't seem like the guards from earlier. For one thing, their helmets were off, and she could see their faces. All of them looked terrified.

Barbara let out another screech as she leapt at the one closest to her. She latched onto his face, arms holding tight while she punched him over and over again with her feet.

Henry picked up a tray and slammed it into the back of

the head of a Sadirian who was lifting his arm toward Barbara. The soldier wasn't carrying a weapon, but the menacing way he pointed the metal bracer built into his uniform made Brigid wonder just what those things could do.

As the man fell, Henry said, "Sorry," then immediately slammed the tray into the face of another Sadirian who was rushing toward them.

The last soldier held both of his arms in the air and backed away from the console in front of him. "Please don't hurt me," he said.

Just when Brigid thought they might have caught a break, one of the doors to the chamber whooshed open. Five soldiers ran in and pointed ray guns at them.

"Tell the Lyrian to go visible and stand down or we vaporize everyone we can see," the first soldier to enter the room said.

"Barbara," Dane said. When she didn't appear, he added, "Please."

Brigid held her breath until she saw a shimmer of white in front of her. Barbara stood on all six limbs, blocking as much of Henry's body as she could. Which wasn't much.

"By order of the High Council, you are all—" The first soldier stopped speaking as a bright light flashed behind her. Four of their group crumpled to the ground, leaving only the one in the back standing.

He stepped forward, bracer raised toward the room.

After a moment, he lowered his arm and tapped the side of his helmet. The metal separated into one-inch segments that folded back on each other, neatly settling into the collar around his neck.

"What?" Brigid gasped.

The man had spiky, light-brown hair, shorter on the sides and back than on top. His eyes were deep blue and his smooth jaw chiseled and strong. He had a straight, narrow nose, and lips that she knew would be full and soft if they weren't pinched into a deep frown.

"Marq," she said.

His gaze snapped to hers. There wasn't a shred of warmth in his eyes that she could see. For all that he and Dane were identical—stubble and scruffiness aside—she could sense the difference in them immediately.

She couldn't imagine what it would take to melt this man's icy veneer. He marched toward Dane and stopped a pace away.

"I came as soon as I could," Marq said.

Dane closed the distance between them, wrapping his arms around the soldier in a huge hug.

"It's good to see you," he said.

Marq's eyes widened a bit. He lifted his arms slowly and patted Dane on the back rigidly.

Okay, maybe Brigid *could* imagine Marq smiling. Eventually.

"You bring strange companions with you," Marq said,

eyeing Barbara warily.

Barbara and Henry were both outright staring. Barbara lifted a hand and pointed from one to the other.

"Are you... I mean..." she stammered.

"I thought the Coalition didn't make clones," Henry said.

"We're not clones." Dane glanced around the room. "So, let's be careful what we all say."

"I suspended the surveillance for this room before my squad entered it," Marq said.

Dane let out a little breath. "Thank goodness for that."

Marq cocked his head to the side as if he was confused by the expression. Brigid realized he didn't have Dane's accent in addition to Marq's weird kind of stilted speech.

"Is Vay here?" Henry spun around, looking at the rooms that were attached to the central chamber. Each held a tank big enough for a fully grown person.

"V-21-b3 is in a separate holding area," Marq said. "I can take you to her shortly, but first, you must call off your soldier who's attacking the ship."

As if to punctuate his statement, a loud *boom* sounded somewhere in the ship. The floor vibrated beneath them and the lights flickered.

"*Our* soldier?" Dane said. "What are you talking about?"

"How about we find our person in one of these pod things first so we can all get out of here?" Brigid asked.

Marq shook his head. "Once the chamber has been activated, the process can't be halted. If you try to remove him now, he'll have permanent brain damage."

"Brendan…" Brigid said.

Henry let out a shaky gasp. "I'm so sorry," he said. "I'm so sorry. God, this is awful."

"How long?" Dane turned toward the one soldier they had left standing before Marq arrived.

The man shook his head. "I'm… I'm not going to help you."

They didn't have time for this. Brigid turned and ducked down, keeping her back toward the soldier. She quickly added vinegar to the powdered concoction she and Henry had prepared, then stood and wheeled around as the mixture began to bubble.

"Tell us what we want to know, or I'll throw this vole rat spit on you!" she yelled.

"Vorrat," Dane whispered.

"Whatever." She lunged forward, smiling as the soldier flinched.

"The process is almost complete," he said. "And you'll all be back in the brig before—"

Henry smacked the man in the back of the head with his now bent-up tray. The soldier crumpled.

"I'm getting less sorry every time I do that," Henry said.

"Is that really vorrat spit?" For the first time since he'd arrived, there was a tremor of emotion in Marq's voice. His face had even paled a bit.

"No, it's a baking soda volcano." Dane shook his head at Marq's puzzled look. "I'll explain later."

"Dane, you have to do something." Brigid set the container on the ground as the reaction fizzled out. "We have to help Brendan."

"There's nothing we can do for him but wait it out," Dane said.

"You need to do something about your soldier immediately." Marq tapped the bracer on his left forearm. A 3-D transparent display of a really cool—and scary— looking ship appeared above it. Several areas were flashing red. "The attacker is heading straight for this chamber."

"They're coming here?" Brigid turned to Dane. "Then it must be one of your friends, right? One of the Vegans maybe?"

"Vegans?" Marq dismissed the display. "There's no such thing."

"A lot has happened since we were last able to talk," Dane said.

"Vegans." Marq raised an eyebrow.

"They're real, and they're here," Dane said. "On Earth. They've already claimed this planet as their new Homeworld, and if the Coalition dares to attack Earth, it'll be war."

"A war the Coalition can't win." Marq's lips tilted up in a grim smile.

Guess I know what it takes to make him smile…

"A war we can avoid," Dane said. "You see how one of their number can punch through our defenses. The *Reckoning* is our toughest warship."

Marq nodded. "This is good. We can use this to stop the High Council from wasting lives pointlessly." He turned to Henry and Barbara. "All our forces have been diverted to repelling the intruder. V-21-b3 is near."

"Her name is Vay," Henry snapped.

"Henry." Barbara reached up and squeezed Henry's hand. "I can find her."

Marq tapped on his bracers a few times. "I've made sure the way will be clear for you and unlocked all necessary hatches between the locations."

Barbara ran toward one of the doors, which whooshed open for her. Henry lingered, though.

"Go on," Dane said. "The sooner we get Vay, the sooner we can get out of here. Brigid and I will help Brendan."

Henry nodded, then ran after Barbara. The moment the pair had left, Marq spoke up again.

"There is no helping the human," he said. "His memory has been downloaded and reset to the month before he made first contact with K-58-b7." Marq paused briefly before adding, "Kira."

A huge boom stung her ears as something hit one of the still-closed doors that led to the chamber. The metal bent inward. Brigid stepped closer to Dane as Marq moved to stand in front of them.

"Don't," Dane said. He grabbed Marq's arm and pulled him back. "If this is someone from the Department of Homeworld Security, you don't want to seem like a threat. Not with the kind of damage they're doing to the rest of the ship."

Marq scowled, the furrow between his eyebrows deepening, but he nodded and stood beside them.

Something hit the door again, then a silver spike smashed through it. Whatever was on the other side of the door used it like a crowbar to pry the door open.

Brigid let out a high, tight laugh. "Maybe you should have unlocked that one, too."

"I was preoccupied," Marq said.

She really hoped whatever this was, it was on their side. The doors screeched open and the Vegan stepped into the room, more terrifying than Brigid had even imagined. It was covered in silver armor, a long tail lashing back and forth behind it. Green light gleamed from the eye holes in its helmet, sparkling off the long claws at the end of its hands.

"I thought you said they were *little* lizard people," Brigid whispered.

"They are." Dane's eyes were wide. He looked as scared as she felt.

That wasn't good.

"That's not a Vegan," Dane said.

It stalked into the room, stopping only a few feet from them. Brigid could see the creature's chest heaving as it looked all around, then locked its gaze on Marq.

The reptilian helmet suddenly segmented, just as Marq's had earlier. The segments folded back on themselves, but only enough to reveal the person's face.

Brigid gasped as she recognized her.

Kira.

"Where's Brendan?" Kira said.

Chapter Sixteen

Dane wasn't sure how to tell Kira what had happened. If she tried to pull Brendan from the mind-wipe chamber now, it would scramble his brain. It might even kill him.

"Where is he?" she demanded.

"We were too late," Dane said. "I'm sorry."

Kira shook her head and took a step back, but something blocked her path. Her brow furrowed as she glanced behind her and saw that the tail of her Vegan exosuit had connected itself to the control console. She twitched her hips, but the tail stayed connected.

Kira had been having trouble learning how to control her exosuit. It looked like she might *still* be having trouble with it.

The lights illuminating most of the side chambers dimmed, leaving only one visible.

"He's there," she said.

The tail of her exosuit retracted, coiling and flattening against her leg. Dane followed her as she ran to the sub-chamber, Marq and Brigid close behind them.

"Kira, wait," Dane said. "You can't pull him out."

They stood before the large programming pod, Kira's gaze searching the surface. He had no idea what she was looking for.

"How far along is the process?" she asked.

A yellow light at the top of the chamber flashed white. Dane's mouth went dry.

"It's done," he said.

Dane had always been terrified of losing Marq to a reprogramming session—whether it was in a mind-wipe chamber, a programming pod, or the seeming safety of their own regen beds. But this... This was so much worse.

He couldn't help but imagine how he'd feel if Brigid had been stripped of her memories of him. They had only just met, and already the bond between them was so strong.

Kira and Brendan had been together for months. They were pair-bonded. Brendan had even been talking about having an Earth-style wedding for them once Kira learned how to use her exosuit.

It was too late for all that.

"I am so sorry," Dane repeated.

Kira's lips pressed into a line so tight, he could barely see any color to them. Her face had paled as well. Much more disturbing, her exosuit's faceplate kept starting to close, then opening back up again. Back and forth, as if she couldn't make up her mind about it—or it couldn't decide what to do for her.

"Kira, you have to calm down," Dane said. "You don't want to lose control of that exosuit."

"I'm not controlling it," she snapped.

Dane's stomach clenched. "If you're not controlling it, who is? The Vegans?"

"No." She shook her head. "I don't know. I mean... I think it's my nanNet."

"NanNets don't act independently of their hosts," Marq said.

"Kira?" Dane prompted.

She kept her silence. He couldn't blame her.

"What's a nanNet?" Brigid asked, her voice gentle.

"Kira is augmented," Dane said. "She had a nanNet installed when she went on active duty. It's a colony of nanites that integrates with a host and boosts their cognitive function."

"That is both cool and terrifying," Brigid said.

Not as terrifying as it would be if the nanNet hadn't integrated and the nanites were doing their own thing—especially with a Vegan exosuit involved. What would nanites even want with the thing?

"Have you lost control of your nanNet?" Dane asked.

Kira glared at him.

She was the only member of the Department of Homeworld Security who had been given a Vegan exosuit besides Ari, and he was Sarah's bondmate. It made sense that the Vegans would trust him with their most powerful and personal technology, since Sarah had become the bridge between Earthlings and Vegans.

Dane had always been curious about why Kira was also given an exosuit—and why she alone had so much trouble mastering it. His theory had been that the Sadirian nanNet wasn't compatible with the Vegan technology. Now, he wasn't so sure.

"We need to know what's going on," Dane said.

"I don't *know* what's going on." Kira spoke through clenched teeth. "Soldiers from the *Reckoning* attacked our Florida base. Sarah, Ari, and the Vegans easily defeated them with their exosuits. I was useless."

"From the look of that door you tore through, I don't think you're useless anymore," Brigid said.

Kira snapped her gaze to Brigid, and the Earthling shrank back.

Dane lifted his hand and gently gestured toward Brigid. "It's okay. We're gonna figure this out." He turned back to Kira. "What happened then?"

"We received a message from Craig," Kira said.

Dane felt a weight fall from him at the news. He felt like he could breathe a little more deeply knowing that Craig really had made it out okay.

"Are he and the nestling okay?" Brigid asked.

Kira's gaze softened a bit. "They're fine. But he... He told us what happened in Montana. That you were all captured." She looked over at the programming pod. "I knew what would happen. I was desperate to get to Brendan. To stop this. I failed."

"We saw you approach," Marq said. "You were flying through the Sol system with just that suit on when you breached the heliosphere. Due to your size, we couldn't get a lock on you before you punched a hole in an airlock, overrode the commands, and started making your way through the ship, stunning every soldier between you and this section."

Exosuits could do that? No wonder the Vegans guarded that technology so closely.

"There is no way anyone could have arrived here faster," Marq said.

Dane's stomach did a little flip as he realized that Marq was trying to comfort Kira. The work they'd been doing to restore Marq's emotions was definitely having an effect.

The programming pod beeped, then unsealed and slowly opened, the front panel sliding around the cylinder and out of the way. Brendan was inside.

He was still in his Earth clothes, resting against the white cushioning designed to prevent damage to the soldiers or citizens unlucky enough to have to go through this procedure. Brendan stirred, blinking his eyes against the bright light of the chamber.

Shit.

With no memory of what had happened, he was basically waking up on an alien spacecraft after being abducted. Dane was close enough to Brendan to know that this had always been a dream of his, but the circumstances were still bound to be unsettling.

"Um… Hello," Brendan said. "This is awkward." He looked around, his gaze fixing on Marq. "Nice cosplay. Very retro."

Marq cocked his head to the side. "Is he speaking Earth English?"

Brendan just laughed. "Someone want to bring me up to speed on the storyline?"

Dane knew about this. Brendan had explained his favorite hobby of creating shared storylines with others, immersing themselves in the tale by dressing up and agreeing on scripts and events beforehand. Sci-fi cosplays were his favorite.

If only this was really a game.

Brendan's gaze lingered for a moment on Brigid, but froze in place when he saw Kira. His eyes widened and his pale skin flushed.

"Hi," he said.

Kira made a few stuttering sounds deep in her throat. She coughed, then said, "Greetings."

Brendan's smile grew. "So, I guess I'm one of the Earthlings, along with you two." He nodded at Dane and Brigid.

"Brendan…" Brigid stepped forward, her hands clasped in front of her. "Do you recognize any of us?"

"No." He glanced around, giving each of their faces a more focused look. He pointed to Marq, then Dane. "Are you guys supposed to be strangers or is your backstory that you're twins separated at birth, with one raised on Earth and the other in space?"

Marq lurched forward, raising his bracer. He'd barely moved before the tail attached to Kira's exosuit lashed out, wrapping itself around Marq's arm. The bracer fizzed and popped, dark smoke coming off of it before the exosuit ripped it away. Marq stumbled backward.

"Kira, stop," Dane yelled. He ran to his brother and gripped his shoulders to help steady him. "Are you all right?"

Marq nodded.

"Whoa, that was cool," Brendan said. "That tail thing…"

"How did you know about us?" Marq demanded.

"What, the twin thing?" Brendan shrugged. "It's pretty obvious… And it's kind of a trope."

Kira's faceplate half formed over her head as she really looked at them for the first time since she'd arrived. Dane could guess what data her exosuit was feeding her.

"You're genetically identical," she said. "But not clones. The DNA markers put in place by our geneticists are missing. That's not possible… Unless—"

Brigid stepped between them, holding her hands in the air. "Hey, let's just go with the backstory Brendan picked out, okay?"

"Are you guys new to this?" Brendan said. "Because you're kind of all over the place."

"You've…stepped into the middle of something," Brigid said.

"I'd like to step *out* of something." He glanced around the interior of the pod. "This set dressing is cool, but it's strange talking to everyone from in here. Plus, I'd really like to get a closer look at that incredible costume you've made."

He couldn't take his eyes off Kira. He leaned out of the pod, but then tilted to the side as if he'd lost his balance. Kira was there in an instant, holding him up.

"Thanks," Brendan said. His cheeks had turned pink again.

Eventually, he would fall in love with Kira again. Dane was sure of it.

He wasn't sure that Kira would ever get over what they'd lost, though. Dane couldn't blame her.

Kira's exosuit folded back on itself until it was just the thick bands of silver on her neck, arms, and legs that Dane was more accustomed to seeing. She was wearing a dark green tank top, shorts, and boat shoes. The Florida base had definitely been taken by surprise.

Of course, Brendan had never seen an exosuit, and from that close, there was no explaining away the incredibly advanced technology. He and Kira were practically embracing—Brendan's arms over her shoulders and hers wrapped around his chest.

"How did you do that?" Brendan asked.

"I..." Kira stuttered, then bowed her head, resting it against his chest.

"Hey, it's okay." Brendan wrapped his arms around her more tightly. "Trade secrets and all. You don't have to tell me."

Brigid was chewing on her lips so hard, Dane was afraid she'd draw blood. Her eyes glittered and she sniffed loudly.

"This is getting a little weird," Brendan said.

He looked around at the chamber with that focused look Dane had seen when Brendan was analyzing things, his gaze lighting on the control console and then fixing on the room outside. The room filled with unconscious soldiers.

"Where am I?" he asked.

"We don't have time for this." Marq stepped away, which gave Dane the chance to go to Brigid.

The moment he touched her, she wrapped her arms around his chest, tucking herself into his side as if she belonged there.

If he lost this—if that had been him standing where Kira was—he wasn't sure he'd be able to keep himself from tearing the whole damned ship apart. And she had the means to do it.

"Brendan, this is going to sound crazy," Dane said. "But you're on a spaceship. A real spaceship."

Brendan laughed. "Very funny."

"Take a good look at the collar around Kira's neck," Dane said. "You just saw what it can do. That's the most advanced technology in the galaxy at work."

Brendan blushed deeper as he brushed Kira's dark ponytail aside. Her hands fisted in the back of his shirt, and Dane felt it like a punch to the gut.

"This can't be..." Brendan shook his head.

Kira finally stepped back from him, but her eyes were locked on the floor. "It can. It is. And you're in danger."

"So, what," he said. "You all abducted me for some reason?"

"Not us, them." Brigid pointed at Marq. "I mean, not *him*, but his coworkers. Co-soldiers. What's the word for that?"

"Brigid, sweetie, you're rambling," Dane said.

She shook her head. "Sorry, I'm just—"

Alarms began to blare, drowning out her words. The chamber blacked out for a moment before the dim emergency lighting came on.

"What the hell is going on?" Dane said.

Marq's eyes had widened, his jaw lax. Of all the emotions Dane had wanted to see from his brother, fear was not one he'd been looking forward to.

"Commander Teisha realizes she miscalculated the threat Earth presents," Marq said. "She's taking us back to Sadr-4."

Chapter Seventeen

"Sadr-4?" Brigid's voice was a high squeak, and she didn't care. "How are the Vegans going to be able to rescue us if we're all the way at Sadr-4?"

"It'll be okay," Dane said. "The nearest dropgate generator is weeks away. The Vegans will have plenty of time to catch up with us."

Dane squeezed her tighter, pressing her against his chest. She held on, willing herself to believe him.

"The *Reckoning* doesn't need generators anymore," Marq said. "I tried to contact you—to warn you. The ship can create its own dropgates into blue space now. That's how we arrived so far ahead of schedule."

"That's not possible," Kira said.

"The Tau Ceti and the Centurans have formed an alliance and worked together to develop new technology," Marq said. "They call themselves the Tau Centauran Assembly."

"You've got to be kidding," Dane said. "Even if they had the resources to come up with this, there's no way the

High Council would let any Coalition planets form an alliance. Pitting us against each other is part of how they hold onto their power."

"They would allow such an alliance if it meant getting access to technology that surpasses their own," Marq said.

Brigid felt Dane still. He wasn't even breathing. She rested one of her hands on his chest and looked up at him.

"You still think everything's going to be okay?" she asked.

He bent down and kissed the top of her head. "I don't know."

"The Vegans were mobilizing when I left," Kira said. Her voice sounded stronger. "And they don't need dropgate generators, either."

"So, we're back at the original plan," Brigid said. "Find somewhere to hide and wait to be rescued."

"Oh, come on," Brendan said. "There are a million things we could do instead. Sabotage the engines. Disguise ourselves as space soldiers."

"I thought you understood that this isn't a game," Dane said.

Brendan shook his head. "The special effects and theatrics are great, but I'm not buying it."

"Listen to me, Earthling," Marq said. "You have been taken aboard the warship *Reckoning* and are en route to the seat of power for the Coalition of Planets—governed by the High Council—which controls most of the known galaxy.

You have been found guilty of founding an unauthorized first contact committee and possession and distribution of forbidden knowledge."

Brendan actually laughed. "Wow, I've been naughty. So, what? Now I go to space jail?"

"The penalty has already been meted," Marq said. "Your memory has been reset to when you knew nothing related to the Coalition, Sadr-4, or the existence of aliens."

"Is this the part where you show me a newspaper with a date on it so I can see how much time I've lost?" There was an edge to Brendan's voice.

"Like we could get newspapers on a spaceship," Brigid said. "It's hard enough to find them on Earth."

She was close to starting to ramble again, and bit her lip to keep quiet. She didn't know what to do or how to help.

Dane stepped forward. "I know you don't remember me, but we're friends. You have a sister named Paige. She's an environmental scientist who worked for Senator Conroy before he was killed by the Tau Ceti."

Brendan's brow furrowed as he glared at Dane. "Jim Conroy is a good man," Brendan said. "You want to go dark with the storyline, fine, but leave him out of this. And Paige."

"It's already happened," Marq said. "I studied General Serath's reports about the events going on with Earth. But this was after you met Kira, so you don't remember it."

"We don't have time for you to not believe us," Kira

said. "Your favorite color is the lime-green of leaves in early spring. Robbie the Robot gave you nightmares as a child."

"I wouldn't call them nightmares, but—" Brendan didn't get a chance to finish.

Kira plowed on. "You tried to turn your mother's vanity into an interocitor in first grade. You prefer apple cider to hot chocolate, Godzilla over King Kong."

He snorted. "Boxers or briefs?"

"Boxer-briefs," she said.

Brendan stared at her briefly, then looked away. "Lucky guess."

"It had nothing to do with luck," Marq said. "Though it's been nullified now, your pair-bond was entered into Coalition record."

Brigid's heart felt like it was being crushed in her chest. She could barely breathe. She touched Dane's elbow, grateful when he wrapped his arm around her.

"Pair-bond?" Brendan said. He looked at each face surrounding him. When no one responded, his gaze returned to Kira and he repeated, "Pair-bond?"

"You and Kira were married," Dane said. "But they made you forget her. Forget everything."

Brendan shook his head and laughed, but there was an uneasiness to it. He shifted his weight from one leg to the other.

"I was married to her." He pointed at Kira. "That's the

least believable thing you've said so far."

"Hey," Brigid snapped, bristling on Kira's behalf.

"Because she's…" Brendan took a deep breath, then let it out slowly. "She's the most beautiful woman I've ever seen. There's no way I'd forget if I was married to her."

"This strategy is failing." Marq strode over to the dashboard-looking thing in the main chamber. He started tapping across its surface, then pulled a cord from his belt and hooked it onto something she couldn't see.

"Marq, wait," Dane yelled.

Brigid's stomach lurched. Suddenly up was down and down was up. She kicked her legs as she floated up from the floor, scrambling for purchase. Dane held her closer against his chest.

"Calm down," he said. "I've got you."

"What the heck is this?" Brigid yelled. Her organs felt like they were all jumbled. She looked back at Marq, safely tethered to what must be the controls for the room.

"Zero-G." Brendan's eyes were wide.

Kira held onto his shoulder with one hand. She arced her body around as the silver bands around her legs expanded into boots. Her feet made a snapping sound as they attached to the ceiling.

"You are on an alien vessel," Marq said. "There is an immediate threat to your life and the lives of everyone else here. There is also a threat to your homeworld if you can't convince the High Council of the legitimacy of the first contact committee you founded."

Marq tapped in more commands. The floor rushed at her, her innards smooshing back together with nauseating speed. Dane landed gracefully on his feet and kept her from hitting the floor. She clung to him as she regained her sense of equilibrium.

Kira was still hanging from the ceiling, upside-down, her ponytail dangling from her head. She was holding Brendan by his armpits and gently lowered him to his feet.

"You all right?" she asked.

Brendan nodded and she released him. He kept watching her with wide eyes as she disconnected from the ceiling with a soft *snap*, flipped around, and landed in a squat on the ground. She stood slowly.

"That was so cool," Brigid murmured.

Brendan swallowed hard. "*We* were married?"

"We were." Kira reached out and clasped Brendan's hand. "And we can be again—if we can figure out how to navigate our current situation."

"I'm sorry, I'm just having trouble wrapping my head around all this." Brendan's voice was thick, his eyes unfocused. "Can my memories be restored?"

Kira's lips pinched into a thin line and she shook her head.

"But you can make new ones," Brigid said. "You can fall in love with her again."

"This is…" Brendan ran his fingers through his hair,

making the red curls stand on end. "This is insane. What the hell kind of people are we dealing with, that they would do this to someone? I mean, our first date? First kiss?"

"The first kiss isn't as important as the last," Dane said. "And if we want to survive with our memories intact, we need a plan."

"No one else is losing their memories." Kira stalked over to Marq.

Dane followed her, keeping his grip on Brigid's shoulders as they walked. Brendan followed.

"Lock down the programming pods," Kira said. "You're the first officer. You have the authorization."

"The moment I use my codes to assist you, they'll know I've been compromised." Marq disconnected himself from the console and gestured to the pile of unconscious soldiers. "Right now, Teisha thinks I'm incapacitated. We need to maintain the element of surprise."

"How surprised do you think she'll be when she sees that the two of you are identical?" Kira said.

Dane flinched. "She won't realize—"

Kira cut him off. "Teisha is a Commander. Her mind has been sharpened, not forced into a stupor like most Coalition soldiers. The High Council wants her to give orders on their behalf, not follow them blindly. She'll see through what you've done to hide your similarities, and she'll order tests that show what my exosuit has already told me."

"And what is that?" Marq asked.

"You're not clones," she said. "You're brothers. I don't know how you were created, but it wasn't in a genetic engineer's lab."

"And that's a bad thing?" Brendan let out a half-hearted laugh.

Dane ignored it. "If they find out—"

Kira cut him off again. "You don't have to tell me what they'll do to you."

"Space jail?" Brendan didn't seem to be trying to lighten the mood so much as reassure himself. His eyes were haunted, and a muscle in his jaw was twitching.

"Mind-wipes and reprogramming," Marq said. "The same as they've been doing to all Coalition citizens for our entire lives."

Dane turned to Kira. "If your nanNet never integrated with you, but it's still functioning, you're in for a hell of a lot worse than a mind-wipe chamber."

"They'll dissect me, down to my DNA," Kira said.

"Wait, what?" Brendan stepped closer to her.

"The exosuit will protect me," Kira said. "I just wish I could convince it to be more helpful."

"So, the nanites the Coalition put in your head are controlling the exosuit?" Brigid asked.

Kira nodded. "I think so."

"But they're good-guy nanites?" Brigid said.

Kira's lips quirked up on one side. It was the closest thing to a smile Brigid had brought out of her. She hoped she would get a chance to do more.

"I suppose you could say that," Kira said.

"Maybe we can talk to them." Brigid looked up at Dane. "Send them a message?"

"They respond to my thoughts," Kira said. "That's why the Vegans gave me an exosuit. They say I'm 'awakened', whatever that means. It's part of some legend."

"Cool." Brendan smiled at her, and even reached out and took her hand in his.

"Can you get them to talk to the ship?" Brigid asked. "See if they can send a signal to the Vegans or help us find a place to hide?"

"With us being on the way to Sadr-4, I don't think hiding is much of an option anymore," Dane said.

"Okay, then." Brigid looked around the room. "We need to meet back up with Henry, Vay, and Barbara. But then we can barricade ourselves in here. Maybe take any weapons those soldier guys have on them in case we have to leave."

"Putting on their uniforms will help us move through the ship if needed," Marq said. "But we lack the time to train you on the use of our uniforms' bracers."

"Just show us how to blow stuff up," Brigid said. The gleam in Brendan's eyes made her think he was eager for some payback.

"Maybe we'll just keep them on the stun setting." Dane squeezed her shoulder. "We don't want you blasting a hole through the hull and spacing everyone."

"Right," she said. "That would be bad."

"This whole thing sounds kind of like a crap shoot," Brendan said.

Kira stepped closer to him. "It's a dangerous situation, but I'll do everything I can to keep you safe." She looked to the others, and added, "All of you."

"The exosuit should help with that," Dane said.

Brendan smiled and let out a soft laugh. "I can already see why I fell in love with you." He brushed a hair behind her ear, then said, "Oh, to hell with it. I only hope this one isn't the last."

He leaned in and kissed her.

Brigid felt her eyes widen. It was so sad thinking of all they'd lost, but at the same time, there was a tiny part of her that was hoping for a miracle.

The metallic bands on Kira's body started glowing. In a pulse of energy that Brigid felt vibrate through her, the bands expanded, enclosing Kira and Brendan in a tall cylinder of light.

Tiny motes of silver drifted away from the pair, clustered as if they were being carried by a breeze. They landed on the console that Marq had been using earlier to control the programming pods.

Dane held Brigid closer. He muttered, "What the hell?" under his breath.

She squinted against the brightness, wanting to see what was happening. Finally, the lights dimmed, leaving Kira and Brendan in the middle of a passionate embrace.

Brigid's cheeks heated. She hoped that she and Dane would get a chance to kiss each other like that again. Well, except for the weirdness with the exosuit.

The couple finally pulled apart—barely—to stare at each other. Brendan blinked a few times, then said, "Kira?"

"Yes?" Her voice was a little breathless.

Brendan looked around, smiling at Dane and Brigid.

"I remember." He turned back to Kira. "I remember everything. How is that possible?"

Kira shook her head, her face beaming with a huge smile. "I don't know. Are you sure?"

"I think so," he said. "I remember my broadcasts looking for aliens and you answering. How you crashed your escape pod into my lake."

"I did not crash it." She scowled briefly. "I set it to self-destruct after a perfectly controlled decent."

"Sorry." He smiled down at her, then kissed her again.

"Not to interrupt," Dane said, "but we have a little problem."

Kira and Brendan pulled apart again. Dane pointed at Kira.

"Your exosuit is gone," he said.

"What?" Kira leaned back, staring down at her body. The silver bands that had adorned her arms and legs were gone, as well as the one around her neck.

"I thought they couldn't be removed," Brendan said.

"That's what the Vegans told me." She ran her hands over her arms as if she couldn't believe what her eyes were telling her.

"What are we going to do without the exosuit to help us?" Brigid said. Seeing it at work had made her feel at least a little more hopeful about their situation.

"Is your nanNet intact?" Brendan asked.

Kira closed her eyes for a moment, then nodded. "I can still feel them."

"That's a relief," he said. "But that still doesn't explain where the exosuit went."

"Could it have gone into that computer thing?" Brigid asked, pointing at the console. The others stared at her. She shifted a little, then said, "That's where the sparkles landed."

"Sparkles?" Brendan said.

"There were small lights coming off of you while you kissed," Marq said. "The Earthling is correct. They landed on the control console and disappeared."

"I have a name, you know," Brigid said.

"Brigid," he said. "I'm aware."

Dane ignored the exchange. "You said your nanites were controlling your exosuit. And that they respond to your thoughts."

"Yes." Kira nodded.

"Why would they have gone into the control console for the programming chamber?" Dane asked.

"The *Reckoning* has different protocols for mind-wipes," Marq said. "We make a copy of all memory cells before wiping them, so that intelligence operatives can review the person's experience for useful or forbidden information."

"I didn't know we had technology that could do that," Dane said.

"You're not supposed to," Marq said.

"The nanites must have figured that out and used it to reconstruct Brendan's memories." Kira smiled up at Brendan.

He picked up her hands and kissed them. "Please communicate my thanks to them."

"Wait a minute." Brigid walked over to the control console, staring at the flashing white lights and strange etchings on its chrome surface. "If the nanites could access that much of this computer, what's stopping them from accessing the rest of the ship?"

One of the flashing lights turned green. No one else seemed bothered by it, but it struck Brigid as strange. All the other lights were white.

"Kira, can you communicate directly with your nanites?" Dane said. "Give them orders, instead of just letting them respond to your thoughts?"

She nodded. "I can."

"But there's a cost," Brendan said.

"It's worth it." Kira closed her eyes again, her brow

furrowing in concentration. "I don't think it's working."

More lights on the console switched to green. The flashing pattern changed as well.

"Am I the only one seeing this?" Brigid asked.

Kira opened her eyes. Everyone looked to where Brigid was pointing.

"The console is malfunctioning." Marq began tapping in commands. "Likely due to the interface with the— Ow!"

He leapt back, shaking his hand. Dane hurried to Marq, inspecting his hand.

"What happened?" Dane asked.

"It shocked me." Marq shook his head. "As I said, the console is malfunctioning."

"No, it isn't," Kira said. "The nanites are still in there. Some of them, at least. I can hear them—and they can hear me." She beamed up at Brendan. "It doesn't hurt to talk to them anymore."

Brendan returned her smile, wrapping an arm around her as they stared at the console. "What are they saying?" he asked.

"They want to know what's next," she said.

Dane looked up at Marq, then over to Brigid and smiled.

"New plan," Dane said. "We're taking the ship."

Brigid beamed up at him. "Now *that* is a great plan."

Chapter Eighteen

Dane resisted the urge to run his hand over his face. His cheeks felt cold without his usual stubble. The back of his neck was even worse.

Were Coalition ships always this drafty?

Brigid walked at his side, fidgeting with the tight-fitting Sadirian uniform she wore. It could barely contain her curves, and showed off every inch of her body. If they pulled this off, he might just get another chance to explore it more.

She caught him ogling her and said, "What?"

He smirked. "Just admiring the view."

"Well, knock it off," she said. "You're supposed to be an emotionally repressed Sadirian soldier."

"Like you weren't checking out my butt earlier," he murmured.

"I'm still getting used to 'the new you'," she said. "I think I like your hair better long."

"Good, because I'm growing it back out as soon as we're done here."

"But I get a kiss before you grow out your stubble again," she said.

He cocked his head to the side, staring down at her.

She shrugged. "I just want to know what it's like."

Chuckling, he turned back toward the corridor. "Whatever you want, sweetheart."

"Watch the pet names," she whispered. "And the accent, too."

Right. He'd have to be careful about that. He set his face in a stern line.

Kira and Brendan walked in front of them, their hands encased in restraints. They all paused at the door to the bridge.

"Everybody ready for this?" Dane said.

Brendan shook his head. "Ready to get it over with."

A light on the access panel next to the door flashed green. Kira struggled to suppress a smile. She looked over her shoulder at Dane and nodded.

"Let's go," he said.

The door slid open, revealing the command center of the ship. Teisha was standing in the center, straight black hair streaming down her back and hands on her hips. Her feet were set in a wide stance as she stared at the viewport.

Instead of stars, swirling, rippling eddies of cobalt and ultramarine blurred past their ship. Blue space.

It had been a while since Dane had traveled using a dropgate. He still couldn't believe the *Reckoning* could create its own.

The Coalition only built dropgate generators near the most important outposts and planets because of the time and resources involved in creating them. The idea that the High Council now had ships that could skip the need to travel to the dropgate generators was unnerving, to say the least.

However he entered blue space, Dane always found the view claustrophobic. Shaking off the sense of all that blue closing in on him, he pushed Brendan's shoulder, urging him into the room. Kira glared at Dane, then followed.

To her credit, Brigid didn't react to the gesture. She kept her face blank as she headed immediately to the communications station, just as they'd planned. No one seemed to notice her.

Dane, they noticed. And not just because he was a head taller than everybody else on the bridge—aside from his 'prisoners'.

Dane nodded toward the soldier who was standing at the communications station. The man nodded back, then switched to another station, giving his over to Brigid.

"Marq." Teisha arched a brow at him as he approached, giving Kira's shoulder a shove this time. "You've returned at last. And with offerings."

"I was unable to provide updates, as these saboteurs have disrupted our communications systems." He kept his voice as flat as possible.

"You look different." Teisha narrowed her dark eyes at him.

"I was exposed to a weapon unlike any I've encountered," he said. "It may have affected me."

"You can report to the med bay after your report." She stepped up to Kira, close enough that their noses almost brushed. "K-58-b7. You have been harboring secrets from the Coalition. I look forward to prying them from your mind myself."

"That may be difficult," Dane said.

Teisha snapped her gaze to his. "Explain."

"She sabotaged the mind-wipe chamber," Dane said. "The technology she used is incredibly powerful."

It wasn't even a lie. Of course, they didn't quite have access to that technology anymore, but Teisha didn't have to know that. Hopefully, by the time they dropped out of blue space, the nanites would have taken over enough systems to be just as helpful as the exosuit—in their own way.

"Where did you obtain this technology?" Teisha demanded.

"As the recently assigned planetary liaison for Earth, I would be happy to answer your questions and act as intermediary with the head of Earth's Department of Homeworld Security." Kira smirked, cocking her head to the side. "Are you interested in establishing a dialogue?

Teisha sneered. "I do not recognize your first contact

committee. And your assignment as Earth's planetary liaison is under review, as all of General Serath's recent orders soon will be."

Dane's stomach sank. It was one thing to suspect that Adam's plan to approach the High Council about Earth's right to establish a first contact committee wasn't going well. It was another to both hear Teisha confirm it and go further.

If Adam's orders were about to be called into question, the High Council must be planning something. Something big.

Adam was the head of the Coalition fleet. More soldiers were loyal to him than the Coalition itself. What were they up to?

If Kira was unsettled as well, she didn't show it. In that calm, low voice of hers, she said, "Very well. If you aren't interested in a parlay, you can return us to Earth."

On cue, she and Brendan both twisted their wrists, making the restraints fall to the ground. It wasn't all that impressive, since they'd never been locked, but Teisha didn't know that.

To add to the effect, Dane leapt back, pointing his bracer at the pair. He struggled to keep himself from faking a surprised expression.

What was living with suppressed emotions even like?

Teisha held up a hand, silently ordering him to stand down. Her frown deepened as Dane lowered his bracer and stood at attention.

So far, their smoke-and-mirrors were working. That was what Henry had called it when they'd all gathered to create their makeshift plan. Misdirection and distraction, just like with the baking soda volcanoes. Only on a much larger scale.

"I will know where you obtained this technology," Teisha said.

Kira smiled. "Earth."

"Impossible," Teisha said. "Earth isn't sufficiently advanced to create anything on this level."

"Earth is a beautiful planet," Kira said. "It's filled with wonderful, welcoming people and very *attractive* resources."

Teisha angled her head. "I see. And who exactly did these resources attract?"

"The Vegans," Kira said.

Teisha's lips curled up in a snarl. "I will not be made a fool of. Tell me the truth."

"I am," Kira said.

"If I may." Brendan leaned forward, placing his face close to the pair. He paused, then in a slightly different tone said, "Is this how Sadirians talk? Because on Earth, this is considered really uncomfortably close."

Kira smiled briefly, then folded her lips between her teeth to try to stop it. She took a step back and nodded toward Brendan.

"Hello," Brendan said, stepping fully between Kira and Teisha. Once he'd insinuated himself, he maintained a distance that was more similar to what Dane had observed on Earth. "I'm Brendan Sloan."

Brendan held out his hand in the customary Earth greeting. Teisha ignored it.

"No?" Brendan said. "Well, that's okay. We can teach you about the different cultural protocols on Earth eventually. You're going to need it."

He smiled and looked around the bridge. "You have a great ship here. Really impressive. Of course, I like the Life Ship better. The Vegans have this wonderful way of incorporating spaciousness and nature in their crafts. Sadirian builds are… Well, they're kind of stuffy."

"I do not believe your ridiculous claim," Teisha said.

"That's fine." Brendan nodded. "I get that Sadirians mostly believe what they've been programmed to. I've been in one of those pods, by the way." He was glaring at her now and he did step in close. "Funny how I seem to remember everything you tried to take away from me, even *after* a mind-wipe."

Teisha's lips twitched, but she didn't say anything.

"I don't think you should try that again," Brendan said. "But I do think you should take us back to Earth."

Just as soon as the nanites have breached the engine and navigation controls.

Dane wondered how Marq and the others were faring on

their missions.

Communications were impossible while they were in blue space—just another way they were cut off from the rest of the universe while traveling this way. But the moment they dropped into regular space, Henry and Vay were ready to send a message back to Earth letting everyone know what had happened. The Vegans would know where they were and would come for them.

The nanites had already prepped and secured the communications channel, making sure no one would be able to detect or intercept the message as it went out. They were chewing away at engine controls now, learning the navigation systems so they could plot a course back to Earth and turn the ship around as quickly as possible.

Marq was in engineering with Barbara. As long as Dane didn't contact anyone down there, they could keep each separate group of soldiers convinced they were both working with Marq. The engineers had no reason to think that Marq wasn't just doing an inspection or working on something for Teisha.

Coalition soldiers weren't used to questioning the chain of command. For once, Dane was grateful for that. It was letting Marq be in two places at once, effectively.

Marq and Barbara would stall anyone who tried to report the drop sequence initiating, giving them time to lock in their course. And if anyone decided to try to sabotage the engines to stop their escape, Barbara would use her unique talents to take care of them.

Brigid had the easiest—and possibly most dangerous job of all. She would stand on the bridge, in plain sight, while watching the communications station. She wouldn't report any alerts she saw from any of the systems they were hacking into and would try to angle herself so that no one else noticed them either.

But while they could control communications to and from the bridge, if Teisha ordered the few soldiers right in the same room with her to open fire, there would be no stopping it.

"I will be taking you before the High Council," Teisha said. "They will decide your fate."

"Nobody decides my fate but me." Brendan shrugged and smiled at Kira. "And my wife."

An alert sounded from the navigation station. Not communications. Dane held his breath.

"Commander Teisha, we are preparing to leave blue space," the soldier said.

Marq had warned them they wouldn't have much time. Dane only hoped that everything was ready.

Teisha nodded toward the soldier and said, "Proceed."

The swirling blues slowed down, then began to fade. Familiar stars burned through the colors as they returned to normal space.

"We have reached the heliosphere of the Gamma Cygni system," the navigator said. "Approaching Sadr-4 at base speed plus three."

"Increase to plus seven," Teisha said. "I wish to return home as quickly as—"

Another alarm sounded. Dammit, had they been discovered?

Dane looked over at Brigid. She glanced at him briefly and shook her head. No alerts from in-ship. This was from outside, then.

"Report," Teisha demanded.

"I am unable to ping Sadr-4," the navigator said.

"Impossible." Teisha gestured toward Dane. "Assist your incompetent soldier in his task."

What a charmer.

Dane walked to the soldier's station, tapping in the commands he barely remembered from his initial training. Marq would know exactly what to do, but it took Dane a while to get the sequences.

"Sir," the soldier said. He glanced up at Dane, stricken. This guy wasn't one of the soldiers in the suppression program, Dane would bet.

"It's okay," Dane murmured.

"But it isn't," the soldier said. "The signals from our navigational relay aren't bouncing back."

Dane remembered learning about the satellite systems that circled the Sadirian homeworld and the space stations that filled the Gamma Cygni system. Not only did they help with communications, they also allowed ships to perfectly triangulate their approaches when they were traveling at high speeds in system.

Of course, most ships didn't have a semi-intelligent network of nanites infiltrating most of their systems. If they looked into it deeper, his group might be discovered.

"Make a guess," Dane whispered.

"Sir?" The navigator's eyes widened and sweat beaded on his upper lip.

"You know this system, right?" Dane said. "Use what you know and plot the best course you can."

"At this speed—"

Dane cut him off. "Do you really think Teisha will be happy if we have to slow down because you can't ping the satellites?"

The soldier's face blanched. "No, sir."

"Just do your best and…" Dane shook his head. "Try not to hit anything."

Dane took a deep breath and blew it out before standing and turning around. He hoped his face looked as calm as he was striving for.

"Well?" Teisha prompted.

"It's addressed." Dane looked past Teisha to where Brigid stood. For a moment, she turned toward him and smiled. Hopefully, that meant something was going right.

Teisha glared at Brendan and said, "You will soon witness what true technological power looks like, Earthling." She tapped on her bracer, changing the viewport.

Stars swept past, but closer objects dominated the screen. Just inside the heliosphere, Gamma Cygni was ringed by an asteroid belt. Dane didn't remember it being quite so thick or dense, but he hadn't been back in a while.

Finally, the screen cleared, giving them a view of space.

Space. Not Sadr-4.

"Report," Teisha demanded.

"I... I don't know," the navigator stammered. His hands were flying across his controls. "It should be right in front of us."

Plasma fire rocked the ship, nearly knocking Dane to the ground. The viewport flickered with purple light. A triad of ships sped past, their triangular design making Dane's heart race.

"Cygnus X," Kira said. "The Tau Ceti are attacking our homeworld."

Chapter Nineteen

Brigid didn't know what to do. She was torn between watching the communications station for blinking lights that might cause them problems and looking at the supercool video screen that was filled with what looked like could be their ultimate demise.

"They wouldn't dare," Commander Teisha yelled.

The ship rocked again, sending Brigid staggering into the wall. Her shoulder slammed into the metal hard enough to make her yelp in pain.

"Brigid!" Dane ran across the room, grabbing onto her. "Are you all right?"

"I'm fine, *sir*," she said, trying to remind him to keep up the ruse.

"Where are our shields?" Teisha yelled. "Marq, what are you doing?"

"Shit," Dane hissed.

"Let me guess," Brigid said. "Marq is the one who takes care of that."

Dane glared at her for a moment, then turned and said,

"Activate the dispersion arrays. Ready weapons."

Thank God he knew what he was doing. For a second, she wondered if med-techs had any idea what first officers were responsible for.

"Nothing is responding, sir." The soldier who spoke sounded panicked. Brigid wasn't far from joining him.

Three of the triangular ships appeared on the view screen again. They were heading straight for the *Reckoning*. Yellow lights shot out from the points facing the ship, each one causing an impact that threatened to knock her off her feet again.

Dane pawed at her belt, grabbing a line like the one Marq had used earlier to tether himself to the control console back in the mind-wipe chamber. Dane attached the line to a small hook next to the communications station.

"Marq," Teisha shouted.

Another ship entered the video screen, completely filling it as it put itself between the *Reckoning* and the attacking Tau Ceti. It was spearlike, with huge spinning gun ports firing beams of white light. But none of the blasts hit the *Reckoning*.

Brigid saw flashes of light on the edge of the far side of the ship. Was it protecting them?

"Serath." Teisha's voice was filled with venom.

Dane started running his fingers over the etchings on the wall in front of Brigid.

"Kira," Dane said. "You have to unlock

communications."

"You." Teisha wheeled around at Kira. "What have you done to my ship?"

"It's not your ship anymore." Kira closed her eyes. Another blast hit the ship, but without nearly as much force as earlier.

Teisha lifted her hand, pointing her bracer at Kira. Time seemed to slow.

Brigid saw Dane lift his arm as well, but knew he wouldn't be fast enough. Brendan was leaping in front of Kira, arms spread.

A bright light flashed in the room, temporarily blinding her. When she blinked her eyes clear, Teisha was crumpled on the floor.

Brendan stumbled a few steps forward, then shook his head. "What just…"

Brigid looked past him, to the navigation officer. He was standing with his arm still pointed in Teisha's direction, his left hand hovering over his bracer.

"I just…" the man said. "I've wanted to do that for a really long time. And now, there's nothing left to lose."

"What do you mean?" Dane said.

"Sadr-4 is gone, sir." The soldier gestured toward his station. "That's why I couldn't ping the satellites. Everything's gone."

Dane started to weave unsteadily on his feet. Brigid grabbed his side to steady him.

"It can't be gone," Dane said.

"He's right." Kira's voice was colder than usual. "All we're detecting is debris and various starships. Every celestial object in the Gamma Cygni system has been destroyed."

Another voice sounded in the room, staticy and distorted at first. A man's voice.

"*Reckoning*, this is General Adam Smith of the *Arbiter*. Have you regained control of your vessel?"

"We have control," Kira said.

There was a pause, then the voice said, "Kira?"

"Affirmative, sir," Kira said. "We've taken control of the *Reckoning*. What are your orders?"

"Take out as many of these bastards as you can," Adam said. "Protect the smaller ships—especially those evacuating survivors."

"Sir?" Kira's voice cracked on the word.

"You have your orders," Adam said.

Kira responded more strongly. "Yes, sir."

The *Arbiter* moved away on the screen. Brigid's stomach did a little twist as she turned back to her station, not sure what to do or how to help.

A green light caught her attention among all the flashing white lights.

"Just like in the mind-wipe chamber," she said.

"What?" Dane looked down at her, but his gaze barely seemed to focus on her. He looked like he might be in shock.

She had a feeling there were others who could help her at the moment, though.

Here goes nothing.

She took the leap of faith and tapped the glowing green light.

Henry's voice sounded in the bridge. "We sent the message."

"The nanites have a favorite color," she murmured.

"What's going on up there?" Henry sounded panicked.

"There are all these ships attacking," Brigid said. "Kira called them Tau Ceti."

"What?" Henry's voice was loud enough to snap Dane back into action.

"Stay put," Dane said, angling his face toward the wall. "The Tau Ceti don't stand a chance against the *Arbiter* and the *Reckoning* together."

"Didn't you say the Tau Ceti had made some kind of leap with their technology?" Brigid wished she could remember the conversation better, but being in the middle of an alien firefight was distracting her. "They were trading it to have that alliance or something?"

"An alliance that they immediately used to launch an attack." At first, she thought Dane had spoken, but then she realized it was Marq's voice coming from somewhere on the wall.

"I'm targeting one of the larger ships," Kira said. "It

looks more like a Centauran vessel."

A sleek red spaceship filled the video screen. It was as big as two of the Tau Ceti ships, but nowhere near the size of the *Arbiter*. White beams of light zapped toward it from the *Reckoning*. Brigid held her breath.

The light flared against an energy field well beyond the hull of the ship. It didn't look damaged at all.

"They've upgraded their shields." Kira's brow was furrowed, her eyes pinched shut. "I can't get through."

"Then how can we defeat them?" Brigid said.

A calm voice sounded over the communications channel. She recognized it as Adam. They must be keeping a line open.

"Our focus is on running interference," he said. "Keep the enemy vessels distracted and focused on us so our smaller ships can reach the dropgate."

"Yes, sir," Kira said.

"Open a channel for me that the Tau Ceti and Centauran can hear." Brendan put his hand on Kira's shoulder. "I have an idea."

Kira opened her eyes long enough to look at him, then nodded and closed them again. "It's ready."

"Tau Centauran Assembly," he said. "This is Brendan Sloan of the Department of Homeworld Security. We represent the interests of Earth and the Vegans and are prepared to enter this altercation to assist the Coalition. Stand down, or be destroyed." Brendan tapped Kira's shoulder. "End transmission."

Kira shook her head. "That was your idea?"

Brendan shrugged. "What else are we going to do? Besides, it's true. When Sarah hears about what happened here, she going to do something about it."

"We have no idea when the Vegans will arrive," Dane said. "Or if they're even coming."

Kira's head jerked toward the video screen. The red ship suddenly flashed out of sight. A few of the small triangular ships sped across the screen. Another large red ship joined them, and they all disappeared as well.

"Did that actually work?" Brigid said.

"With good reason." Kira nodded toward the screen, her eyes wide.

Two large white vessels came into view. They looked like upright nautilus shells surrounded by daisy-like petals at their base. As Brigid watched, the petals detached themselves and headed off in different directions.

The screen flickered, the darkness of space replaced with a bright room. Brigid didn't notice anything in the background. She was too busy staring at the bright green face in the center of the screen.

"Little lizard people…" She was seeing her first Vegan. She sucked in a breath, then murmured, "It's so cute."

Dane leaned close and whispered, "They don't like it when you say that. Especially Cerulean."

Lucky for her, the lizard person on the screen was

focused on other things.

"I am Cerulean, acting Voice for the Vegans," he said. "Be at peace, Sadirians. At the request of our Protector, we are here to assist you."

The screen split, another face joining Cerulean's. This one belonged to a gorgeous man who Brigid was almost certain was Sadirian. Aside from his supermodel good lucks, he had one impossibly green eye and one that was an equally brilliant blue.

"Greetings, Cerulean," the man said. "I am General Adam Smith, formerly designated as Serath. We are honored to accept your offer of assistance."

Brigid finally felt like she could breathe again, though she was far from feeling safe. She put her arms around Dane and pressed her face against his chest. He hugged her tight, kissing the top of her head.

"Is it over?" she mumbled.

"No," he said. "Far from it."

"I've switched to a secure channel." Kira cast a withering stare at the four Sadirian soldiers who were still on the bridge, including the one who had stunned Teisha. "I've reviewed your files and believe you'll be able to make the adjustment to the new chain of command. Am I wrong?"

"No, sir," they said in unison.

Kira nodded, then turned back to the screen.

"How bad are the losses?" Cerulean immediately asked.

A muscle in Adam's jaw twitched. "Not as bad as expected. We discovered that Sadr-4 was largely depopulated. The High Council hasn't bothered to replace citizens on the homeworld for the last several centuries. They've been keeping the planet to themselves."

"You're kidding me," Brigid said, a little louder than she intended. Okay, a lot louder.

Adam fixed his gaze on her and she shrank back against Dane.

"Forgive me," Brendan said. "This is Brigid. She's my new chef."

Adam sighed. "Of course she is."

"A noble profession." Cerulean actually bowed his head briefly. "Our Protector has also dedicated herself to nourishing her brethren."

Dane whispered, "That means she's a chef, too."

"Cool," Brigid said.

Adam continued with his report. "Most of the casualties came from the space stations and domes. The Tau Centauran Assembly has effectively destroyed every habitation we had in Gamma Cygni. It's as if they weren't interested in eradicating us so much as destroying our home system."

Cerulean was quiet for a moment, his head bowed. "We, too, have suffered the loss of our home system," Cerulean said. "We will assist you as much as we are able."

"Thank you." Adam nodded gravely. "The Coalition has

many colonies. We will review their populations and see which can support additional citizens until we can build more stations and dome worlds."

"What about our system?" Brigid asked.

Everyone turned to look at her. She did her best not to shrink against Dane again. Instead, she straightened. She held onto his hand, though.

"There are places in our solar system that can be colonized with your advanced technology," she said. "We're already working together. Is there a reason we can't be neighbors?"

"It is a generous idea, but—" Adam was cut off by a cute blonde woman who popped into view on the screen.

"We'd absolutely have to run it past the Department of Homeworld Security first," the woman said. "Oh wait, I'm one of the founding Earthling members, and I vote 'heck yes.' And I can already think of a dozen locations that would be great for dome worlds."

Brendan chuckled. "I can think of quite a few myself, but I'm not the astronomer." He nodded toward the screen. "Hey, Evelyn."

"Hey, Brendan." The woman waved. "It's nice to meet you, Brigid. Especially if you're not a health-food chef. No offense to the great Protector of the Vegans."

"Um…thanks?" Brigid said. "And my specialty is molecular gastronomy. I like to study food."

"If we could stay on topic," Adam said.

Evelyn cast a tight-lipped smile at him. "We all handle stress in our own way, and you know I tend to ramble, and now that I'm married to the guy who's in charge of the whole freaking galaxy, I'm just a little bit freaked out."

"In charge of the galaxy?" Dane said.

Adam let out a sigh. Evelyn actually looked a little abashed. She put her hand on his shoulder.

"I'm sorry," she said.

Adam clasped her hand and held it. "We have confirmed that every member of the High Council was on Sadr-4 when the planet was destroyed."

"The *entire* High Council?" Kira said.

Adam nodded. "We had been ordered to remain in the system while they deliberated on our requests about Earth."

"How does that make you in charge of the galaxy?" Brendan asked.

"According to Coalition law, if the High Council is incapacitated in any way, the highest ranking officer in the fleet takes command," Adam said.

"And that would be you." Evelyn gently pressed her head against his.

"I see." Cerulean's scaled lips pulled into a smile. "Then this could be an opportunity for all of our peoples."

Adam nodded. "We're damned well going to make it so."

Chapter Twenty

Dane wiped sweat from his brow. More moisture beaded on his back and ran down his spine, plastering his shirt to his body. He closed his eyes, lifted his face to the warmth of the sun, and smiled.

"I've never seen anyone enjoy the heat like you do." Brigid's voice broke his reverie—not that he minded. Especially when she had a huge glass of lemonade in her hand. "You need to stay hydrated."

"Thanks." He took the glass and downed half of it in a go, then set it on the workbench next to him.

"You cut your hair again," she said. "And shaved."

He ran his hand over his cheek and smiled. "Guess I did."

Brigid narrowed her eyes at him. "Why?"

"Secret mission."

"What secret mission?"

"If I told you, it wouldn't be secret."

She scowled at him, then shook her head. "You've got to stop visiting the *Reckoning* disguised as Marq."

"You know I can read his crew's emotions better than he can."

"I guess. I like your hair longer, though."

"Then I'll grow it out again."

She smiled at him as he picked up a sheet of metal and placed it against the frame for the wall he was working on.

"Don't you have like robots or something that can do this work for you?" she asked.

"You forget, I'm a hands-on kind of guy."

He grabbed her waist and pulled her up against him, prompting her to squeal and swat at him. They both ended up laughing.

"You're all hot and sweaty," she said.

"And I'd love for you to join me."

"How about I join you in a shower after Sarah and I finish getting dinner ready for everyone."

"Let me guess." He cocked his head to the side as if thinking. "Baked beans over spaghetti?"

"Gross. No. We're having our first real cookout. So, we'll both really need that shower later."

"Good, because I love having an excuse to be very thorough when washing you."

He claimed her lips for a kiss that started with her giggling and ended with them both breathless. If the building he was working on was just a little farther along in construction, he'd find a secluded spot and—

A high chittering broke into his thoughts. He turned to

see Sis and Sister standing off to the side, an iron beam held between them that would have crushed him and a dozen Sadirians if they'd tried to lift it without an antigravity unit. The Antareans weren't breaking a sweat.

Not that giant ant-people ever broke into a sweat.

"Do you need to leave early today?" Sis said, her huge segmented eyes strobing pink as she picked up the pheromones he and Brigid were no doubt putting of.

"No, he does not." Brigid gave him one last kiss, then pushed off from his chest. "Because *she* needs to finish dinner for everyone. It's not easy feeding a base filled with Sadirians and Lyrians and Antareans and Vegans and... Is that everyone?"

"There is a Scorpiian," Sis said. "And the Tau Ceti Alan and his half-human offspring."

"And also many cats," Sister added, as the pair walked away.

"It's a lot of mouths to feed," Brigid said.

Dane nodded. "And a lot of roofs to build over them."

"We all have a lot of work to do," she said.

"I'll take the Earth-side work over what Marq's doing any day," he said.

Dane shuddered at the thought of overseeing construction of the mining operation and new colony on the far side of Earth's moon, in addition to building the new space station in LaGrange point L2. All while bringing the crew of the *Reckoning* in line.

Of course, Adam was working on most of the sentients in the galaxy, while fortifying defenses in case the Tau Centauran Assembly decided to strike again. Maybe Marq wasn't that bad off after all.

"Is Marq coming to dinner tonight?" Brigid asked.

"No, he's stuck on the ship."

"I worry about him up there by himself."

Dane grinned. He couldn't help it.

They'd made so much progress restoring Marq's emotions that Dane knew his brother was ready for the final missing piece in the puzzle. Someone—or *something*—to love.

"What's that grin about?" Brigid asked.

"Just… Don't you worry about Marq being alone," Dane said.

She narrowed her gaze at him. "I know that smile. You're up to something."

"Then I guess you better keep a very close eye on me."

He grabbed her again and pulled her in for a kiss, taking his time and enjoying the feel of her, the taste.

When he let her up for air, she said, "I intend to. But after dinner."

She ran her hand down his arm as they parted, giving his hand a final squeeze before walking away.

Everyone had their own part to play in the future they were building together—the Coalition and Earth. From chefs to generals to med-techs turned construction-workers.

Together, they would make something brighter than ever before. Something new.

Dane turned back to the sheet of metal he was securing to the framework for the habitation unit he was building, knowing in his heart that he was finally home.

Epilogue

The instant Marq stepped into his quarters, he knew that something was wrong. He held perfectly still as the door shut behind him, surveying the Commander's quarters he had only recently acquired.

The chair in front of Marq's personal workspace was turned at a different angle than he'd left it. Someone had been in the room.

Marq activated his bracer with a subtle movement of his left hand, sensors sweeping the area for explosives. It had only been a few Earth months since the Tau Centauran Assembly had destroyed Sadr-4 and the High Council along with it. Marq would not be their next victim.

His bracer beeped, letting him know without looking, without moving, that the room was clear of immediate threats. His nerves remained taut, body and mind ready to take action.

Scans could be wrong.

Stars filled the viewports above the cushioned couch and chairs in the decadent sitting area across from him—except for the section of space taken up by the far side of Earth's moon. Though currently in darkness, the moon's surface was speckled with lights.

Progress was swift setting up staging areas for construction of *Outreach*—the Coalition space station that would become the central gathering place for his people. He couldn't understand how some Sadirians could wish to sabotage their efforts, holding on to a vision of the Coalition that had died along with the High Council.

Marq headed for his sleeping chamber, intent on scanning everywhere to ensure the safety of himself and the ship. *His* ship.

As he passed the workstation, one of the monitors activated, displaying a familiar face.

"Hey there, bro."

Marq froze, his chest tightening with an unfamiliar sensation.

"Dane," Marq said.

It was still novel to communicate openly with his brother. Not long ago, their talks would have been clouded by the threat of discovery—and the penalty of mind-wipes for both of them if others became aware of their unique connection.

"You have a minute?" Dane asked.

"My rejuvenation cycle is beginning."

"Great," Dane said. "Have a seat."

Marq spun the chair around, balking when he saw a

small life form on it. No, not a life form. It was an inanimate object, but made to look like an animal.

He reached down to pick it up, grasping it by its tail and holding it closer for study. It was made of soft fabric, with round ears, tiny black eyes, and short hairs sticking out from its muzzle.

"Did you infiltrate my ship again?" Marq said.

"Infiltrate?" Dane laughed. "No. I was just making a delivery."

No deliveries were scheduled within several Earth solar cycles. *Days*, Marq corrected. His crew would check in with him about unexpected arrivals—unless they already believed they had.

Dane normally wore his hair past his ears, and let his stubble grow more than Marq could ever tolerate. At the moment, Dane's face was smooth and his hair was cut short on the sides and only slightly longer on top. It was styled exactly as Marq wore his own.

"And did my crew know who they were addressing?" Marq sat. He suspected he knew the answer.

Dane shrugged. "I never said I was you. I just told them I was still getting used to the layout of the *Reckoning*, and they were kind enough to point me in the direction of your quarters."

"The biometric scanners couldn't differentiate between us well enough to keep you from entering?" Marq asked.

Dane's smile pulled more strongly on one side of his

face—a smirk,—revealing straight, white teeth.

"Why would the Coalition need to make their security that granular when they don't make clones?" Dane said.

"Or allow people to have twins."

Dane's smile dimmed. "Yeah. There's that, too."

"You could have asked." Marq rubbed at his chest, trying to loosen the tight feeling there. "You're welcome on my ship. And we could have spoken face-to-face."

"I miss you, too," Dane said. "But I was 'up to something', as Brigid would say. I didn't want you to say 'no'."

"Say 'no' to what?"

Dane grinned broadly, cocking his head to one side. "I, um... I left you something."

Marq lifted the fabric figurine. "I noticed."

"No, not the mouse. That belongs to Meredith."

"Meredith?"

"Yeah, she's in the other room."

Marq's mouth suddenly dried. The tightness in his chest gave way to a fierce pressure that caused him to feel every beat of his heart.

"Relax," Dane said, leaning closer on the screen. "I'm not trying to get you to pair-bond with anyone."

The pressure lessened, resulting in a lightness in Marq's head that made him dizzy. He gripped the table to steady himself.

"This may not have been a good idea," Marq said.

"Just breathe." Dane took in a huge breath, then let it out slowly, gesturing for Marq to do the same.

After a few breaths, Marq said, "Perhaps we should wait until the space station is complete to finish restoring full access to my emotions."

"Or we could wait till the war is over. Or until we've brought Earth's governments into the Department of Homeworld Security." Dane shook his head. "There's always a reason to wait."

"The timing for this is not ideal."

"I know. But it's too late to go back. We've already changed the programming in your regen bed. The barriers our scientists put in your brain are almost all down."

"We began our work before I became Commander of the *Reckoning*," Marq said. "Or was charged with building *Outreach* station and keeping Earth safe while the Tau Centauran Assembly is handled."

"I get that." Dane was quiet for a moment, then said, "You know that Brigid has a twin sister. Caitlin."

"You've mentioned this."

"Since Brigid and I pair-bonded, she's been telling me all kinds of stories about their bond," Dane said. "I want that bond for us. I want us to finally be brothers."

"We already are brothers."

"I know, but we haven't... We haven't bonded like they have." Dane shook his head. "I guess I'm being selfish, wanting more."

"If wanting to feel a strong sibling bond makes you selfish, then I am, too," Marq said.

A large smile spread across Dane's face.

"That's why I think this will work," he said. "'Want' is at the root of so many emotions."

"Right now, I want to know who Meredith is," Marq said.

Dane's enigmatic smile prompted a strange mix of emotions in Marq that he recognized as unease and excitement.

"Not who," Dane said. "*What.*"

—

Thank you so much for reading *Coalition Reckoning!* I've been working on this story for years—almost as long as I've been writing the series. Bits and pieces would come to me while I was writing the novellas, letting me hint at what was to come. I knew that *Coalition Reckoning* would need more space on the page (see what I did there?) and really enjoyed spending that extra time with the characters and their world. I hope you enjoyed it as well!

Now that we've seen behind the curtain with the Coalition, we'll be spending more time on ships, space stations, and more. But the stories will always be grounded on Earth and in the hearts of the hero and heroine finding their "Happily Ever After."

But for now, let's see what sort of surprise Dane has left with Marq aboard the *Reckoning*. Read on for an excerpt from the next book in the series, *Import Quarantine!*

Import Quarantine

The Department of Homeworld Security
Book Eleven

Chapter One

A green blur filled Caitlin's vision. She blinked a few times, bringing the face of her clock into focus.

"Two o'clock in the morning," she mumbled. "Why am I awake at two o'clock in the morning?"

Someone pounded on her door, loud enough to make her bolt upright.

"That would do it," she said.

"Caitlin? Caitlin O'Rourke?" The voice echoing through her house was loud, male, and sounded desperate.

Caitlin jumped out of bed. The clothes she'd been wearing yesterday were piled on a chair next to her dresser. She pulled on her jeans and a T-shirt so she wasn't running around in her pajama shorts and tank top.

"Weapon. Weapon. What can I use as a weapon?" She spun around, looking for anything she could defend herself with in case he broke down the door.

"I need your help," he shouted.

She paused her frantic search.

If someone needed help badly enough to track her down in the middle of the night, something terrible must have happened. Or maybe something terrible was *about* to happen, just as soon as she opened the door.

If she went and talked to him, he might at least stop pounding on her door. At this rate, he would knock it down without even meaning to.

"Please," he yelled. "I need a doctor."

"Craaaap."

She grabbed her phone from her bedside table and ran to the door, stepping up on her tiptoes so she could see through the eyehole. The motion sensor light had tripped, and through the fish-eye lens, he looked...

Pretty cute, actually.

He had greenish-blue eyes, sandy brown hair—shorter on the sides than on the top—and a strong jaw and nose. Nice lips. Really nice lips. His arms were braced on either side of the doorframe and his shoulders were broad enough that he looked totally capable of knocking down her door.

"Wow, he is buff," Caitlin whispered.

He lifted his fist and hammered on the door again, hard enough to make the pictures on the walls shake. She yelped and jerked back.

"Caitlin O'Rourke!"

"I'm here," she yelled. "You can stop knocking."

His tone hadn't lost any of its urgency when he said, "I need your help."

"I'm not a doctor."

He went quiet.

She was about to look through the eyehole again when

he said, "Brigid told me you were."

"Brigid," Caitlin murmured. "Of course."

Brigid, the quieter twin who somehow lived the more interesting life. Brigid, surrounded by celebrities that hired her to cook for them. Brigid, the valedictorian, who could do no wrong in their parents' eyes.

"I'm a veterinarian," Caitlin said.

"A what?"

"An *animal* doctor." Caitlin raised her voice so he could hear her clearly.

"That's what I need. Please, my cat needs help."

His cat?

She looked through the eyehole again.

The lens distorted his features, but she could still see the anguish in his expression. Why had Brigid sent him to Caitlin, though? Where was he even from?

He couldn't be local. The town was too small and Caitlin would definitely have noticed him.

"I need you to come with me," he said.

"Oh, no, no, no." She laughed as she spoke, her nerves getting the best of her—and making her speak loud enough for him to hear. Plus she was still looking through the eyehole, so her mouth was pointing right at the door.

"Why not?" he said. "Isn't it your job to help animals in need?"

"I have got to stop talking to myself," she hissed. Hanging around animals all the time had firmly entrenched the bad habit.

Loudly, she said, "I'm not going somewhere in the middle of the night with some strange guy that I don't even know."

No matter how hot he is.

"I'll protect you. You have nothing to fear."

"That's exactly what someone who wanted to kidnap me would say."

He shook his head. "What does *kidnap* mean?"

"You're not helping your case. Everybody knows what *kidnap* means."

A few moments passed while he messed with his watch.

"That's… Cygnus X, that's awful," he said. "I don't want to kidnap you. I want you to come with me."

"And I don't want to come with you. Hence, *kidnapping*."

"I'm not going to—" He pinched his eyes shut, then took a deep breath, expanding his already impressive chest. After holding his breath for a few seconds, he slowly let it out.

"Call Brigid," he said. "She knows you can trust me."

"Call Brigid," Caitlin mumbled in a mocking tone, but she was already dialing the number.

She didn't expect Brigid to answer, really. Her sister's latest client was keeping her busy. He'd moved her from Montana to Florida along with the rest of his household after only a couple of weeks in his employ. Apparently,

Brigid was already indispensable.

The client must be a big deal. Brigid wasn't even allowed to tell Caitlin who she was working for.

"Caitlin?" Brigid answered before Caitlin had even heard the phone ring.

"Weird…" Caitlin mumbled.

"Are you okay?" Brigid said. "It's two o'clock in the morning where you are."

"I'm aware," Caitlin said. "But there's this huge guy pounding on my door. He says he knows you."

"Wait, what?"

Caitlin looked through the eyehole again. "Six-foot something, light brown hair, chiseled jaw…soulful blue eyes."

"Dane?"

Caitlin held the phone against her chest, and yelled, "Is your name Dane?"

"I'm Marq. With a 'Q'." His voice trailed off as he added, "Brigid said…people make assumptions."

Caitlin lifted the phone and said, "He says his name is Marq. *'With a Q'.*"

"Shit," Brigid said.

Caitlin perked up. Brigid never cursed. *Never.* This guy must be bad news.

Or *big* news. Like somehow involved with whatever secret celebrity Brigid was working for.

"Let me talk to him," Brigid said.

"Why?" Caitlin turned to lean her back against the door as they spoke. "So you can cut me out of the conversation?"

"This isn't the time—"

"No, it isn't. And it hasn't been for months now." Caitlin hated how rough her voice sounded. She hadn't realized how raw she was over this. "You're my sister. My twin. We don't have to share everything, but since you landed this new job, it's like you're shutting me out of your life."

"I'm sorry you feel that way," Brigid said. "And I get it. I really do. But there's more going on than you know."

"That's exactly my point!"

"Just, let me talk to him," Brigid said.

"You want me to open my door to this guy in the middle of the night? Because I was considering calling the police."

"Don't call the police!" Brigid nearly shouted.

"I see," Caitlin said. "So, I can trust him."

"Of course you can, but—"

"That's all I needed. Bye, sis."

Caitlin disconnected the call and quickly set her phone to *do not disturb*. She took a deep breath, then turned and opened the door. "Okay, so you need help with your...eep!"

Her gaze slowly rose from his booted feet, up along his muscular calves and past equally sculpted thighs. His T-shirt was tucked into his cargo shorts, showcasing his perfect waist. She could see the outline of his abs through the thin fabric.

His shirt clung to his chest, accenting strong pecs and shoulders she wanted to jump up and hang from. And his face…

Dear God, his face.

The chiseled jaw was even better than she'd imagined. Straight, strong nose. Lush, sculpted lips. Pensive brow, drawn together above those soulful eyes.

He was perfect. Impossibly perfect.

"I… Are you…" He stammered, then pointed behind himself. "Are you ready to go?"

"Hmm, what? Oh. Right." Caitlin shook herself. She had a patient who needed her help. "I need to grab a few things from my clinic."

She started by picking up her wallet and keys, then slipping into her sneakers before stepping out onto the porch. Instead of backing away to give her space, he just stood there, staring down at her. She leaned over to close and lock the door, doing her best not to bump into him— even though she really wanted to bump into him.

She slid her wallet into her back pocket, then gestured toward the path that led to her clinic.

"After you," she said, and not at all because she wanted to see if the back side of him was as gorgeous as the front.

He nodded curtly, then turned and headed down the path. Caitlin stood on the porch for a few moments, watching his long gait.

"Oh my God," she whispered. "It's just as gorgeous."

—

About the Author

USA Today Bestselling author Cassandra Chandler uses her vivid imagination to make the world more interesting, spawning the ideas she turns into her whimsical Science Fiction romcoms and darkly evocative Paranormal and Urban Fantasy Romances. Fast-paced and funny, lighthearted or dark, her stories will introduce you to characters you want to be friends with and worlds where you'd like to build a vacation home.

www.ingramcontent.com/pod-product-compliance
Lightning Source LLC
Chambersburg PA
CBHW071312250626
47159CB00004B/1397